James Gould Cozzens (1903–1978) was born in Chicago and studied at the Kent School in Connecticut and at Harvard University. He left Harvard to devote his full time to writing, and over time his career was distinguished by critical and popular success. His novels include *Men and Brethren, The Just and the Unjust, Guard of Honor* (for which he won the Pulitzer Prize), and *By Love Possessed.*

. . . how infinitely good that Providence is, which has provided in its government of mankind such narrow bounds to his sight and knowledge of things; and though he walks in the midst of so many thousand dangers, the sight of which if discovered to him, would distract his mind and sink his spirits, he is kept serene and calm by having the events of things hid from his eyes . . .

THE LIFE AND STRANGE SURPRIZING ADVENTURES
OF ROBINSON CRUSOE OF YORK, MARINER.

JAMES GOULD COZZENS

Castaway

ELEPHANT PAPERBACKS
Ivan R. Dee, Inc., Publisher, Chicago

CASTAWAY. Copyright © 1934, 1962 by James Gould Cozzens. This
book was originally published in 1934 and is here reprinted by arrangement with Harcourt Brace Jovanovich, Inc.

First ELEPHANT PAPERBACK edition published 1989 by Ivan R. Dee,
Inc., 1332 North Halsted Street, Chicago 60622. Manufactured in the
United States of America.

Library of Congress Cataloging-in-Publication Data
Cozzens, James Gould, 1903–1978.
Castaway / James Gould Cozzens.—1st Elephant Paperback ed.
I. Title.
PS3505.099C69   1989   813'.52   89-35468
ISBN 0-929587-17-0

CASTAWAY

ONE

The Ascent into the Store

Supported against the stair rail, Mr. Lecky might have been sick; but his stomach was empty. When he retched, all that rose was a bloodwarm lump—perhaps his heart bounced on the firm spurt of his terror. With this throatful, and the nausea it caused him, and the unmanageable shaking of his body, Mr. Lecky's utmost mental feat was to recognize, as finally he did, that he had reached the basement of the department store.

Panting, trying to swallow back his heart, not for a full minute could he notice what might be noteworthy: the dim, dismal illumination shed by infrequent small electric bulbs, with a world of shadows depending from pillars and massed counters; down the receding empty aisles, the subterranean silence. Since he could not see anyone, Mr. Lecky began, fearfully, to listen.

In his own head he felt as much as heard a ringing, painful and persistent, like the last of a loud detonation or stupendous jar; but Mr. Lecky was not confused. The sound that he was trying to hear would be running footsteps, the brush or bump of a quick search for him. What he would do if he heard it, Mr. Lecky did not know. In despairing anticipation he feared to hear as much as he feared not hearing anything. To be pursued and know it was hardly better than to be pursued and not know it; yet he listened. The shadowed, wanly electric-lit vast silence pressed on him as though he were sunk in a pond of quiet. Silence was so perfect that he became suddenly aware of his own breathing— hoarse regular gasps as good as signals of his whereabouts. Thinking of that, he thought, too, that this stillness lacked some right or natural quality. He did not believe that it was the empty quiet of desertion. Far from empty, it seemed full, as of great stealth or patiently prolonged motionlessness. Compelling his aching chest to hold in lungfuls of air as long as possible and loose them quietly, Mr. Lecky turned his congested, dreadful face from side to side. Several times not comprehending, staring with stupid furtiveness, his eyeballs sticking half paralyzed on each shift, the excruciating edge of his listening unrelaxed, he beheld the long table nearest the foot of the stairs.

Its surface was covered with many shapes and sizes of kitchen knives in shining rows. Mr. Lecky continued to look at them, nipping his tongue with his teeth. Stirred then, but not with really conscious volition; not going, so much as strongly drawn, he began to move. Four steps took him across the aisle and he snatched a knife from the table. The wooden hilt was set with almost a foot of broad, never-used keen steel. Clutching it, he wheeled about, to see who was watching him.

He could see no one. There was nothing in sight and no more sound than before; yet his impression of something happening, some important change in progress,

4

had been no illusion. The light had a different tone. The yellowish quality of its color was being cut shade by shade; thin shadows were in general rising movement. First distrusting his eyes, Mr. Lecky looked directly at the bulb on the nearest wall. Every instant the frail incandescent filaments glowed more distinctly in their own lessening light.

Mr. Lecky sprang for the stairs. He got his left hand on the rail. Gripping the knife to his breast, he started in a lumbering frenzy to run up; now two, now three steps, now stumbling, for the precipitate gloom ended sharply in total darkness. Gaining the landing, he did not stop, but he faltered. Pallidly down the broad opening to meet him, he found, astonished, the gray light of dawn; and at once his mind fabricated for him a curious reassurance. Automatic devices which turned off electric power when a certain degree of natural light reached controls somehow sensitive to it undoubtedly existed. What had made him run was the thought of a hand stretched out to throw a switch. Machines were something else. They knew neither hate nor murder; they had no heads full of urgent desires or bloody, incalculable plans. Mr. Lecky flung himself on. At the top he glanced up and down the wide twilit aisle. Turning sharply aside, he hid crouched against a counter to see if anything came up after him.

Just as downstairs he had listened hard, all the while desiring with great anguish not to hear anything, he must wait now expectantly for what he hoped not to see. Downstairs he might not have heard; but here he would be able to see. No one could come quietly enough to be invisible. As seconds amounted to minutes and one minute followed another, the pain of crouching tormented Mr. Lecky's calves. Driven at last beyond care by it, but with his legs now too exhausted to rise, he fell forward, thudding down on his knees. This sound, it seemed to Mr. Lecky, must be audible from end to end of the great main floor. He did not look to see what came of it. Acting as though it had not happened, he breathed on laboriously. At random he thrust his hand into his pocket, took out his watch. It showed quarter past five.

The information was of no value to him. Turning his eyes aimlessly, he gazed through the glass side of the counter against which he knelt. Like all those near enough to be seen in the growing light, it contained silverware. Sidelong, with torpid incuriosity, Mr. Lecky stared at the enclosed trifles: miniature pots and bowls for salt; shakers for pepper; sauce boats, bonbon dishes, sweetmeat baskets; tea caddies topped with colored finials; cream jugs; engraved vinaigrettes of no special use. Looking at all these things slowly and stupidly took some time, and suddenly Mr. Lecky grew impatient. Nothing could exceed the folly of kneeling here, not-looking his only defense . Still holding the knife, helped by the counter edge, he got himself to his feet. Seeing nothing and hearing nothing, he began to walk, quickly and carefully, away from the stair head in the silverware department, down the broad aisle toward the outer doors.

The doors—there were ten of them set side by side in one long heavy metal frame—were locked. Mr. Lecky's hand was halted by an oblong of plate glass. Looking through, he could see the spacious dusky vestibule divided by a collapsible grill, drawn across and fastened in place. Beyond this strong steel lattice he could make out the line of doors on the street, all their narrow shades pulled down. Getting out this way would be difficult.

Mr. Lecky faced around, his back to the doors. Here, at least, he was better off. His corner commanded the cross avenues of the aisles; his back was secured. He could, of course, himself be seen from a distance, but his absolute surprise would not be easy to effect. Lifting his eyes to the source of the slowly growing light, he saw the big semicircular window tops fifteen feet or more above a man's head. If, below the exact arc of the arch, they were real windows, the frames were covered up by woodwork descending to a point within ordinary reach. Here began multiple tiers of closed drawers.

Suppose, Mr. Lecky hazarded suddenly, he were asleep, dreaming. Dreaming, sliding into the monstrous fantasies of nightmare, he had surely felt this very breast-pressing weight of danger, made efforts to awaken, prove to himself that he was all right and nothing impended. The relief, the hope that he might open his eyes in his bed could not be accepted. He was without any doubt awake already.

Aware once more of that ringing in his ears, though it was fainter now, he tried again, his mind at work slowly. Suppose then that he had somehow injured himself and lost his memory. This was a sickness or accident of which he had often heard. People ceased to know who they were, where they came from, or even where they were going. The idea, while useful and plausible, did not satisfy him. He knew clearly that he was Mr. Lecky. He said to himself: *I remember that when I looked at my watch it was quarter past five.* Taking his watch out he looked at it and saw that he was right.

Mr. Lecky had been growing calmer, but this demonstration that he was all right, in the sense of really being where he appeared to be, and of knowing it, served to start again minute cold crispations of the skin on his shoulders. The fears he had formerly felt of hearing, and then of seeing, seemed to have changed a little. He was aware, unreasonably, of a reluctance in his perplexity, like a fear of knowing; or a resistance to it, as though he were half persuaded that what he did not know would not hurt him. Whether only in the realization of his own mind, or in the deadly clarity of the demonstrated event—an enemy given time to catch him, or the sudden sight, the taking-in, the abrupt comprehension of something in plain sight but understood too late—an explanation was perhaps not what he wanted. Mr. Lecky looked at his knife. Though it was a large and dangerous one, he got little comfort from it.

To Mr. Lecky's left, eight elevator shafts were closed by metal doors. Halfway down, affixed to the wall, he could see light reflected from a sheet of glass covering what must be the store directory. The sight of it roused him with fresh plans and improved ideas. Walking carefully, looking carefully for any sign of opposing movement, at last he turned his back on the widespread floor, began hastily to read down the long columns of white letters.

Whether he remained here, or found a means to leave, he ought certainly to possess himself of the best possible weapons. By the term Mr. Lecky understood some sort of firearm. The fact that he was totally unacquainted with the use of guns assisted him in the illusion that, given a revolver, he would instantly become formidable. Trusting machines as he did, he regarded a revolver as a small killing machine. He believed that its operation required little more than pointing and pulling a trigger. The revolver would obediently deliver, unerring and fast as light, death to a great distance.

Revolvers, Mr. Lecky found at once, were not listed here; but his reading, continuing, passed over ribbons, rubber goods, rugs, and stopped on the words: Sporting Goods & Outing Supplies. The generalization gave him immediate hope. Outing would surely mean hunting—so important a reason for a man to deliver himself to the discomforts of improvised living in the field. Hunting would be impossible without guns.

If guns were there, they would be found on the eighth floor, and the sooner he investigated, the better. He would, Mr. Lecky said to himself, run right up there. Accustomed to doing this figurative running in elevators, Mr. Lecky did not realize to what a degree seven flights of stairs like those he saw behind doors at the end would tax him. He was, however, incapable of operating an elevator, even if power to lift it were available. Looking one last time about the main floor in the light of almost broad day, he pushed open the pair of swinging doors. He walked to the stairs and began to climb with impressive confidence.

One flight (no more than he was occasionally used to) had him breathing faster, for he was in a hurry. He paused a moment on the landing, less to recover himself than to consider whether he ought to make an investigation of these large floor areas he planned to pass. On the whole, he thought, no. Until he had armed himself, the last thing he wanted was to find anyone. He began more slowly, with an unwelcome sense of no retreat necessarily assured, to climb once more.

At the next landing his legs were paining him in calf and thigh. Standing for a moment to ease them, Mr. Lecky found his apprehensions on the increase. He did not like the white light of the windows whose great oblongs were sealed with a glass fused in blurring corrugations over a wire netting. He was shut in and well enough lighted, but he could not see out. With him he had nothing but the kitchen knife, pushed awkwardly through his belt. No number of weapons on the eighth floor could help him here. Shaking himself a little, he began to climb, pausing every step or so to hold his breath, look about him in the blank ample light, listen, rest his legs. Thus he came to the third landing and was confronted fairly with a weapon better at least than a kitchen knife. Against the wall, its handle in one bracket, its blade in a wider one, hung a great scarlet axe. For use in case of fire, it was simply waiting there to be taken. Mr. Lecky went and took it.

Here surely was the sort of axe they fought with in medieval battles. More than a yard of some tough wood formed a handle which was anchored solidly with wedges in a steel head. It was painted scarlet, except for a narrow seven-inch arc of sharp blade edge. The other side had been molded to a spike. No skull could stand up against that; its point would sink easily to the core of a man's brain. Mr. Lecky regarded the axe with appreciation, but he none the less could not help feeling its unhandiness. To raise it and strike it against wood or a wall might not be too difficult; to direct it at a moving opponent was another matter—for him, probably impossible. Mr. Lecky made a move to put it back; but even as he lifted it he was again impressed by the long helve, the murderous head, the bright alarming color. Swung on his shoulder it was a load, but anyone seeing him coming so equipped might not be sure that the axe was beyond his power to use. He began to climb once more, the helve against his neck, the keen blade (like a gun, an axe was an instrument he had never learned to handle) at a perilous angle behind his head. Thus, with augmented labor and straining breast, he gained the fourth floor.

Mr. Lecky's natural impulse was to sit down on the steps a moment; but, starting to do it, he could not conquer an instinct to keep his face toward that approach which would give attack the impressive advantage of impetus from above. Not that it would be impossible for somebody to bound silently, far faster and more easily than he himself had come, up from behind. He half wheeled merely at the thought, his back to the strip of solid wall between the white windows; but he saw that no such thing had happened, nor was it about to. In any event, with luck, his axe might be effective in that direction, while in the other so useless as to make flight his only hope. The thought of flight disquieted him, since he had failed to arrange for a retreat. Attempting one, the lower floor doors to the stair shaft could at any instant swing open to cut him off. Having alarmed himself with these possibilities and dangers, Mr. Lecky decided that it would be better to sit down, if he must, on the halfway landing above where the stairs doubled back on themselves. Though he was not rested and the pounding of his unprepared heart made his stomach sick and his sight uncertain, he climbed on.

Attaining his trifling objective, Mr. Lecky was giddy. To teach him less ambition, he seemed to taste blood in his mouth. The axe, removed from his shoulder, was too heavy to hold. It struck the floor of the landing with a clash, horrible and warlike, filling the whole shaft with the clangor of steel on steel. Supported between the unsteady helve and the rail, Mr. Lecky sank leadenly on his buttocks, unable to make any preparations to defend himself from whatever responses might come to the still-echoing advertisement of his presence. He rolled his head against the thin iron posts of the rail, gulped down air jerkily. Sweat slid off all over him. Waves of hot, distinctly red-colored vibration swam across his eyes. The throb and hammer of his head excluded thought unless a despairing awareness that he was not yet much more than halfway up could be called a thought.

After a long time (there was real sunlight now against the glass through which he could not see) Mr. Lecky moved again. It was, he found, overwhelmingly necessary for him to empty his bladder; and though he supposed that he might find, if he looked, some proper and decent place to do this, his exhaustion was too great for him to seek it. The act irked and disgusted him, yet he must perform it where he was. When he was done, he moved on as promptly as he could, for putting the results out of sight repaired somewhat the grossness of his impropriety. So stimulated, the excess of his effort took him to the fifth floor, and almost to the next midway landing. Here he lay in aggravated prostration for perhaps ten minutes.

Reason would suggest that after the preliminary grievous effort of getting to his feet, progress on them would be faster and easier; but when Mr. Lecky came to move again, he did not attempt to stand up. Neither did he discard the axe, which by no possible exertion could he have lifted or used. In the extremity of its exercise his will held no traffic with reason. He began, simply, step by step, to crawl, dragging the red axe with him. Thus in time he reached the sixth and seventh floors; and in more time, groaning and slobbering, the eighth. Here he lay long, defenseless, on the open landing. The worst that could come to him was death and he would not mind it. He might have fainted or slept, for with much vague time passed, he felt somewhat stronger. In the end he was enough restored to stand, assisted by the rail, erect.

A preliminary survey of the unknown floor which Mr. Lecky purposed now to enter might be the part of prudence. Hardly and so newly able to stand up, Mr. Lecky saw the uselessness of petty precautions. Though on his feet again, the great axe still in his hand, he could neither fight nor flee. He leaned his shoulders against the doors, which promptly swung open, nearly letting him fall. Staggering, he saw that he was in the toy department.

The association of ideas which accounted for the arrangement of goods in a store like this appeared reasonable, being familiar, to Mr. Lecky. The gaiety of this half acre of playthings was even comforting. He was not dismayed. No wagons conquering plain and mountain to jolt at last into an Oregon ever found vaster relief or simpler joy. Mr. Lecky stood a moment, resting again, while he examined this goal of his.

Here among the toys, the pillars supporting the ninth floor above had been made to look like irregular piles of children's blocks. Mammoth, as much as a yard square, they bore on some faces an enormous colored letter of the alphabet, on others, an Arabic numeral, or one of the conventionalized pictures of such everyday animals as elephants and giraffes. Around these pillars, under the additional innocent decorations of the painted walls, it was not easy to imagine danger lurking.

Mr. Lecky walked on slowly, his axe over his shoulder, through parks of velocipedes, tricycles, down lines of small red-wheeled carts and sleds with light iron runners. Four hundred square feet of table-top bore a jumble of motionless toy trains on endless circles of weak silver-colored tracks. Beyond, another such surface supported lead soldiers: companies, troops, batteries, uniformed by every nation for every war of the world's last three thousand years. To please more practical or less imaginative children, followed counters piled with things to build or put together: miniature airplanes, motorcars, boats, large boxes packed with unconvincing bits of metal meant to be structural steel.

Animals in wood and wool and rubber, of every size and approximate shape, came next. Dolls, Mr. Lecky saw, looking left, occupied shelves along one whole wall. However, Mr. Lecky was getting to where he wished to be, for now appeared the various balls and sticks, the special garments and uniforms worn by children old enough to play games in teams, needing organization. At this stage they were, too, sufficiently inured to life to amuse themselves in the dirt and damp of the fragmentary poor woods and rubbish-filled coverts of nearby countrysides without necessarily fatal results. The progression, more rapid, became one of enlarging the clothes, making heavier and stronger the implements for play. On small platforms, covered under foot with a shaggy green stuff representing grass, several sorts and sizes of tents were pitched. Beside them, colored canoes lay on bowed and swollen flanks; small rowboats turned up their light varnished planking. Mr. Lecky walked quicker, shifting his axe to the other shoulder. He saw frail palisades of fishing rods behind counters whose glass-enclosed depths were strewn with open packets of false, hook-concealing flies and gleaming with reels. There in the corner resting, muzzles in blue steel ranks against the green baize lining of the closed cases, were the guns.

The cases were locked. Mr. Lecky hesitated. Then he lowered the axe, holding it waist high in both hands. He let it swing gently forward and the whole sheet of glass fell to fragments at his feet. Gripping the axe, Mr. Lecky turned in a spasm to see if that splintering crash had attracted any attention. Then he leaned the axe against the counter behind him, reached through the door frames and lifted out the gun at the end of the first row.

Had the question been put to him, Mr. Lecky might have known that some difference existed between a rifle and a shotgun; but there had never been any occasion for him to discriminate between them. What kind of gun he held, or what ammunition he would require, he did not know; but he was almost satisfied merely to hold any gun in his hands. The enormous hardship of the climb, like his judgment, was justified. He felt already master of the whole building.

Laying down his beautiful gun, he finally set about the search for cartridges. They were not so labeled, but the drawers behind the counter against which his axe stood seemed a probable place; and since they, too, were locked, his axe would again be required. He was afforded small room to swing it here, and a pointless, instinctive caution made him at first strike gently, no more than indenting the wood with the steel spike. When, with timorous reluctance, he hit harder, it was still a moment before he could burst open the first drawer. Lifting it out he tipped the contents carefully on the floor. Squatting, he examined the heaps of clean, heavy little sealed cartons.

A simple feeling for order made Mr. Lecky soon guess that the number with the decimal point probably referred to size. He began to arrange the boxes in sequence of caliber, from .22 to .303, putting aside perplexing irregularities like 25/30, 250/3000, and boxes declaring the contents of .300 Holland & Holland magnum rimless, or, impressively, 7.62 m/m Russian Military Bronze Pointed. With some sixteen varieties laid out, he slit the paper sealing on the at last useful point of his kitchen knife and prepared to try the cartridges one after another until he found those that fitted.

Mr. Lecky now encountered a difficulty at once ridiculous and formidable. Unless he were to drop these metallic cartridges down the muzzle (plainly the wrong procedure), he could find no immediate way of getting them into the gun. No doubt something ought to be pressed, turned, or pulled to give him access to the breech. He began patiently to work at every joint or projection.

Forced to observe the gun he held with care—indeed, with dawning anxiety—he saw on the barrel where it met the inflexible breech the engraved words *"Fabrique Nationale d'Armes de Guerre Herstal Belgique,"* which was plainly no direction for opening it. To Mr. Lecky these foreign words were an unpleasant discovery, suggesting a necessarily inferior weapon, and he sat still, no longer even trying to open it. He was, in fact, holding a Browning automatic twelve-gauge shotgun, complicated by magazine cutout and double extractors. For this, naturally, none of the ammunition he had laid out would serve.

Even attacked halfheartedly, the obduracy of the gun, unaffected by his pressing and pulling, soon had him sweating. It was—he began to see it some time before he could let himself admit it—hopeless. Laying the gun at last on the floor, he felt what might soon be panic. Any courage and pleasure which had first been his presupposed loading to be a trifle, quick and easy. Mr. Lecky got to his feet, hastily bringing out guns that looked in any way different and so perhaps simpler. He even produced exactly that express bolt-action sporting rifle which, had it been explained to him, he would have recognized as what he had vaguely in mind. Now, while he deduced from the small muzzle that it was more likely to take the sort of cartridges overflowing their open boxes around him, the complexity of the breech mechanism looked greater even than that of the Belgian shotgun. Picking up new guns and discarding them, Mr. Lecky worked with increasing carelessness. Employing a gun butt, he smashed the glass of the second case and produced a staggering fresh load. Only when he had worked over the last of these and laid it down in consternation, only when he found himself helpless amid some forty firearms, did the idea of printed instructions occur to him.

Snatching his axe, Mr. Lecky began to break open everything within reach that was closed. The situation seemed too desperate for temporizing, or for consideration about quiet. He swung his exhausting axe without plan or system, hit again and again until the drawer-fronts split everywhere and fell to pieces. Out spilled cartridge belts, leather and canvas gun covers, cleaning rods, swabs, scratch brushes, flannel wipers in packages. Other drawers soon proved to be full of special sights, telescopic mounts, wind-gauge combinations. Sometimes more than drawers were broken. Out issued trickles of Rangoon oil, of strong-smelling solvents for copper and nickel fouling. Crushed and severed sections of tubes containing gun grease and rust remover fell to the floor. Now, too, he began to find the larger square boxes of game loads. Torn open, they showed him red, yellow, violet, green paper shotgun shells and he saw, distracted, that they must be meant for the larger muzzled guns.

Turning in fury, looking for something still unbroken, Mr. Lecky noticed on the far counter corner a heap of small booklets. He let his axe go and, taking one in his damp, unsteady hands, read INSTRUCTIONS FOR PURCHASERS on the cover. Exasperated to have raised such havoc in search of something all the while in plain sight, his fingers pressed open the pages to which they contributed grimy smears and found for him diagrams keyed with numbers, illustrations making clear the loading and cleaning, even aiming and firing.

Mr. Lecky fell on his knees looking for weapons made by the issuer of the booklet. With one such gun across his thighs, the diagram flattened out beside him, he accomplished the simple miracle of releasing the breech-bolt. Fumbling through the discovered boxes of ammunition, he filled his hands with red shells and fed them into the magazine. He closed it and locked the breech. He leaned back against the side of the counter, breathless and triumphant.

TWO

The Armed Man

ARMED, HIS ENERGIES
enough restored for further action, Mr. Lecky was
astonished to see by the changed direction of the light
through the windows that morning had become early
afternoon. This made him think of food. With immediate savage suddenness his stomach spoke to the same
end. During the terrors and exertions of the long fore-
noon his belly must have been resigned. Except for exhaustion's occasional quakes of nausea, it had remained
mute, not disturbing him while he was busy with more
important matters. Now he must satisfy it. He must
look for the grocery department.

Very hungry though he was, and half convinced as he
was, too, when he considered it, that the ordeal of the
stairs had been in large part due to lack of food, mere
possession of his gun put him in a more calculating
frame of mind. Sooner or later he would need, even
more than food, a place to sleep which would be as safe
as he could make it. Immediately another consideration
occurred to him. This stock of arms and ammuni-

tion ought to be safeguarded. It would be the most dangerous sort of negligence to permit any other prowler, who might, like himself, be originally unarmed, as easily to repair the deficiency.

Looking about him, impatient for an idea which would free him to eat, Mr. Lecky's eye fell on a group of fitting-rooms in the section devoted to sports clothing. This structure consisted of six closet-like compartments where customers might retire to try on the garments hanging ready for them in the nearby cases. Although it stood perhaps a yard higher than a man's head, Mr. Lecky could see through an open door that it was not roofed over. Presented with this concrete problem, he thought at once of knocking out the hinge pins from the doors. Doors would do very well, once loose and at his disposal, for making a platform on top. By moving thither his guns and cartridges, and what food he might need, he would have a citadel, if not impregnable, at least fairly commanding and proof against surprise.

Pleased by his plan, he could even consider a moment the advisability of making the arrangements at once. He decided not to. His present hunger and weakness might make the task of removing and raising the doors and carrying all the guns beyond his strength.

Amid the surrounding wreckage Mr. Lecky noticed and now picked up a belt of webbing fitted with numerous narrow loops to hold shotgun shells. Strapping it around his waist he filled the more accessible openings with the proper ammunition. Taking up the gun, which he held alertly in both hands, he went the shorter distance to the elevators on this side. From the directory posted there he learned that groceries were on the sixth floor; and cheered by this relative nearness, he pushed open the swinging doors with his foot. Into the stair shaft he came cautiously, gun, muzzle first, finger on the trigger. Seeing and hearing nothing, he began his descent, quiet, watchful, but almost sick with hunger.

By gracious accident, Mr. Lecky had picked the side and the stairs which, on the sixth floor, allowed him to step directly into the grocery department. He did not have to pass through the great reaches displaying glass and china which adjoined it. His mouth, as the general faint odor of so much food reached him, was suddenly swimming with saliva. His head swam, too; and, incautiously setting the butt of his loaded gun on the floor, he supported himself a moment by leaning on the muzzle while the ordered tables swung across his eyes.

Most immediately at hand was one side of a bright pyramid of shelves surrounding a pillar. They were entirely filled, he saw, amazed, with sardines. In jars, with olive oil, with lemon, with truffles; French fish in tins; Bordelaise; boneless and skinless Portuguese packings; smoked Norwegian Bristling; sardines in wine sauce, in every shape of tin and glass. Some of these Mr. Lecky could get at quickly since the flat tins were equipped with keys to tear off and roll back the metal tops. He began to snatch them up while he moved in a nervous anguish of greed, disclosing to himself the pyramid's right side. This was black with caviar in glass of descending sizes. Against this side Mr. Lecky rested his gun. Applying a key to a sardine tin, he wrenched back the top, spilling the olive oil in his shaking hands. He dug in with his fingers and greedily filled his mouth with half a handful of broken fish.

The taste of food restored Mr. Lecky from the witlessness of his first snatching. The tin was empty and he put it aside on a table edge. Deliberately he filled his pockets with more tins; for, should he be interrupted, or by some chance find nothing easier to get at, he could always have sardines. Taking up his gun again, he wiped his hand on his trousers and moved on, jaws still busy with his great mouthful.

Perhaps he had been wise to fill his pockets with sardines. All the adjacent displays were of vegetables in glass jars: hills of visible, chill and sodden small beets; thin beans, white or too green; peas poisonously bright, and yellow messes of corn. Eventually these might be valuable, in view of that part of Mr. Lecky's convictions having to do with physiology and health. He believed that it was necessary to include vegetables in his diet, but now he had no time for them.

He had reached biscuits and packaged cakes; and Mr. Lecky gathered up some of the smaller and more convenient boxes. His gun was again a nuisance. He set it down to tear open a package and refill his mouth. Busy with this, he saw through an arch beyond a whole ceiling hung with smoked and wrapped hams. At once he dropped the remaining biscuits. Forgetting his gun, he hastened to possess himself of what he considered proper, solid food. Jerking down a ham, described on its wrapper as cooked, he realized that what he needed now was the kitchen knife, left where he had used it to open the cartridge boxes upstairs. Immediately he remembered, too, his gun; and clutching his prize, he rushed back to get that.

Mr. Lecky would not very soon forget his sensation when he rounded the first of the biscuit counters and found that his gun was not there. He dropped his desirable ham on the floor, frozen in terror too exquisite for any phrase or adequate thought. His hair actually lifted on his head. There was not a sound, nor any visible movement. The gun was simply gone.

He took an undirected step, and another, chiefly to keep his balance, for he did not know which way to flee, nor what to flee from. Doing this, he discovered, almost fainting in reaction, that his gun was exactly where he had left it, behind the second table.

With the blue metal in his icy hands, he stood shaking. He felt that death had brushed by him. He was not wholly certain of the miss. He turned, still trembling, finding the floor in front higher at every step than his foot expected. His fingers hooked on the counter edge, he stooped and picked up the ham. In the same uncertain way he selected a large tin box of biscuits. Carrying both, and the gun, he walked, shocked and stupid, to the doors by which he had entered.

This load was much clumsier than the axe, but sense of a direction already determined, perhaps the few mouthfuls of food which he had thrown his stomach, made it possible for him to climb in his diminishing numbness steadily and quickly. Prying open the door on the eighth floor, he pushed through, ham and biscuit box insecurely against his breast, gun swinging in his aching fingers. The unchanged silence awaited him. Proceeding to the counter where his knife rested, he set down box and ham, propped the gun against his thigh. Ripping the cloth package from around the meat and slashing off the stubborn thick rind at the end, Mr. Lecky cut himself a slab of ham perhaps an inch through. Sparing his right hand now to hold the gun, he sank his teeth into this formidable slice.

*

His hunger finally satisfied, Mr. Lecky looked for water. A white porcelain drinking fountain of the sort which, at pressure on a button, threw up a jet, came promptly to his eye. It stood by the stair doors. As he went toward it he realized that there might be no water in it, or in whatever pipes or tanks fed it. Foreseeing the annoyance of a second trip to the sixth floor for some kind of bottled beverage, he was surprised when the button, pressed, produced the right result. Water leaped freely up and he captured it in his mouth. Fresher now, by contrast, rested, he returned to the cases of firearms and reconsidered his idea for spending the night.

This still seemed perfectly practicable. The first move would be to take off the doors and cover the open compartments with them. Whether the removal could be managed with his bare hands was the one doubtful point. If tools were needed, certainly he could hope to find none nearer than the basement. Tomorrow it might be wise to undertake such an expedition and add a hammer, pliers, a screw driver, to his equipment. Meanwhile he had his axe with which he could probably break the doors from their hinges.

So thinking, absorbed in calculation, he noticed an object fallen from one of the split drawers. It was a loading tool for metallic cartridges, but to Mr. Lecky it looked very much like an unhandy but strong pair of complicated pliers. Taking it, and being careful to bring his gun with him this time, he went over to the fitting-rooms. He applied his supposed pliers to the round head of the hinge pin, managed to manipulate the handles until they held. He jerked. To his great pleasure, the pin gave promptly, lifted out and fell to the floor. The door sagged off, hanging only by the upper hinge.

A chair from inside the compartment now enabled Mr. Lecky to reach and remove this hindrance. Free, the door leaned, and he steadied it while he dismounted. Seeing that his gun was as conveniently close as it could be, Mr. Lecky took the door in both hands, raised it against the upper edge of the compartment wall. Pushing and heaving, he got the door up until it half rested, almost balancing. Hopping and shoving, he moved it farther and farther until, releasing it cautiously, he found that it had reached, landing with a light thud, the other side. There it was.

This operation had proved encouragingly easy, in the sense that he had been able to do it at all; but the necessary incidental exertion made him decide, when he had laboriously put them up, that three doors would be enough. The afternoon was drawing on, and the task of transporting the guns and getting himself settled on his citadel would be no work of a moment. Considering the last point, he saw that he ought to provide something soft for him to sit or lie on, since he would be obliged to do one or the other for many hours—a few heaps of the clothes in the nearby cases would serve. Sliding back the glass door of the nearest case, he helped himself to coats—short, but thickly lined with matted fleece. Having thrown out a considerable pile on the floor, he gathered up an armful. Getting precariously on the chair, he succeeded in lifting and clumsily tossing this collection across the horizontal doors. No more than two or three went too far and fell off the other side. Another armful would do no harm, he decided.

His ham and his box of biscuits could go up next. He could also relieve himself of the sardine tins which had been bulging his pockets uncomfortably. There remained the arms and ammunition.

So many guns would leave no room for himself, and Mr. Lecky had a helpful inspiration. Anyone who needed a gun would need ammunition, too. If he brought over all the cartridges, he could bring only a few guns, to which at leisure, he might fit the proper shells, so if the worst came to some unpredictable worst, he would be spared the helpless pause of reloading.

Time was growing valuable. His watch, he found, had stopped. It still declared quarter past five, and could, indeed, have been correct again; but held to his ear, it made no sound. He might as well assume that quarter past five was the time, wind it, and let it proceed on that basis. When he had done this he went about collecting and carrying over the ammunition. There was a great deal of it, so he spent surely no less than half an hour; but when he had finished and selected his guns, and was ready to get up himself, his watch still said quarter past five. Plainly it was broken and useless. He returned it to his pocket, disgruntled.

By assembling three chairs, seats together in a circle, it was possible to place on them two chairs, facing each other. A little caution in movement would let him climb them. The chairs remained, convenient for someone else to use, but he could no doubt knock them down from above. Mr. Lecky saw no other way at all of effecting an ascent. He was not young enough, and far from athletic enough, simply to lay hold on the high edge, raise himself until he could swing a leg over one of the compartment tops still left open and rise easily erect, straddling the wall.

He could, however, imagine an active enemy doing it. The best safeguard he could think of would be a row of small objects, almost any kind, distributed along the edges. Anyone attempting that approach while Mr. Lecky slept could hardly help knocking off some of these small things and so warning him. Frowning, he took his gun and went in among the toys.

A short search revealed nothing so convenient and so certain to cause a great racket falling as the light metal cars forming the toy trains. Detaching half a dozen of them from their locomotives, he brought them back. Taking down one of his chairs to stand on, he set these toys at intervals on the compartment edges not covered by his three doors. Returning the chair to its previous position, he climbed up.

Once on top amid the unarranged accumulation of his miscellaneous gear, Mr. Lecky found that six doors would have been much better than three. He crouched, in effect, on a little raft whose instability was increased by the careless, uneven placing of what doors he had. The ends of two of them protruded into space, where also they were ready to tilt him and his supplies if any movement of his shifted the center of gravity too far. This he corrected as well as he could, painstakingly moving the heaps of clothes and cartridges and food to leave one after another of the doors clear. Squatting down on the other two, he could then tug the free one into a more secure and orderly position. The double pile of coats he arranged in a low rampart, sorry now that he did not have more. Whatever the actual strength, a wall, even low and of cloth, gave an illusion of shelter. On it the guns could be laid, pointed in various directions, ammunition stacked to one side.

Mr. Lecky had been so absorbed in these adjustments

that the stealthy growth of shadows into a general gloom became only now inescapably apparent. Lifting his head he saw it, and with consternation. His one serious, almost incredibly heedless oversight was demonstrated. All day long he had neglected the matter of lights. The dark coming down was already rendering useless both his eyes and his guns.

The recognition of his carelessness filled Mr. Lecky with fear and anger. In the dusk his eerie heart could anticipate the hours of terror which he had laid up for himself. Sounds, real or imaginary, the silences and secrets of the night, the working of his own mind, skilled in cruel illusion and rich in evil fancy, would find him without recourse.

Here was nothing sitting still could cure, and cured, it seemed to him, it must be. Perhaps, had he not known that electric torches were sure to be available somewhere, Mr. Lecky might have found the mental means to survive without them. Natural resources of brain and nervous system could and would adapt themselves to the inevitable; but they made no compromise with convenience. Only in the last uncontrollable stage did they make one with exhaustion.

If fear, unconscionable, bade Mr. Lecky be up, common sense bade him be quick, undertake his descent into the store while some light remained to help him. He bound on the web belt full of shells. He advanced the loaded shotgun to the edge so that he might reach up and get it from the floor. Then he let himself down.

The stairs were lighter. A pale lucid twilight lay on the steps and landings to hearten Mr. Lecky a little, but very little. Although resigned to the proposition that a light was necessary, and so concentrated on the means to make a light, although harassed by the importance of haste, and the hope of being back soon at his safe base, Mr. Lecky moved reluctantly. He was wearier in bone and muscle than he felt. He went heavily, even thoughtlessly, for he had descended a flight of stairs before he recalled that he had never troubled to learn, from the directory, where he was going.

He was both discouraged and frightened while he halted at the doors of the seventh floor. The unknown reaches which they hid would be dark; he might not even be able to read the directory. Wasting thus moments which he could not afford, he peered finally into the squares of glass set at the level of his face, pushed irresolutely, holding his gun tight, and stepped through. The darkness was not so deep as he had imagined that it would be. He could still see that this part of the floor held heaps of rugs, rolls of carpet. Moving along the elevators, the goods changed to draped upholstery fabrics, dim piles of pillows, rows of false windows set up to display the uses of curtain materials. He could not tell what might be hiding among them, so he did not try. Instead, staring closely at the dim white lines of the directory, straining his eyes, his nose almost against the glass, he learned that flashlights were on the main floor.

Insentient matter, putting itself wantonly as far from him as possible, could not be commanded to come; and if he cursed it, it could not hear or fear him. Slowly, disheartened beyond precaution, Mr. Lecky went out again, on down, not thinking any more than he could help of the climb back.

Arrived finally on the main floor, he found here light almost as good as that dying in the stair shaft. He found, too, that what he sought was close to the stairs, in count-

29

ers immediately fronting the rank of useless elevators. He tried to take heart, for with flashlights he was more familiar than with guns. He could select at once two electric lanterns—squat rectangular cases of olive-green metal whose batteries would not be used up even should they burn for hours. To these he added a long torch. By the size of the bulb, reflector, and magnifying lens, it promised him a powerful hundred-foot shaft. These three would serve very well. He checked them for batteries, bulbs and their proper functioning. Pushing his gun under his arm, hanging the lanterns by the clasps on their back to his cartridge belt, and holding the long torch in his hand, Mr. Lecky turned back to the stairs.

Since he had light, he snapped it on. One of the weighty lanterns sagging at his belt, tilted forward, threw a pool of radiance shaking and swaying on the steps as it jerked and bobbed to his climbing. This was good, and good, too, was the knowledge that he had somewhere to go; but he knew it vaguely only, in an apathy of exhaustion which saw good things after all not very different from bad. So he began the great labor of the climb back to the eighth floor and the security of his citadel.

Mr. Lecky never got any farther than the third floor. Not conscious of impossible fatigue, feeling less than his distress of the morning, he was notwithstanding seized by a faintness. This sudden spinning dizzied him. A darkness as impalpable, more discrete, yet blacker than night's, spun out from dancing points to overlapping disks. They were so wide, so close to his eyes, that he could not strike them off. He had only a second given him to see and apprehend. This same second loosened his grip on consciousness. He seemed to let go, hardly struggling. His muscles let go everywhere, too. He had time to hear, like some remote accident, the bang of the shotgun, gone, the smash of glass in at least one flashlight lens. This was the thin segment of the actual second, and Mr. Lecky knew nothing of himself slumping to lie on the stairs with the things he had dropped.

THREE

The Fortification of the Lavatory

Following its outraged failure, Mr. Lecky's body, though unused to sleeping on steel, made no effective protest. Its discomfort could not penetrate the stupor enwrapping him. At most there was a twitching of muscles, the gradual performance of movements which completed his slipping, carrying him to a more satisfactory rest on the level landing. He had lain without concern for ten hours when strengthening light on the fused glass aroused him. His eyes opened.

Reduced temperature and cramped circulation squeezed pain from all his joints as Mr. Lecky tried to move. Without, that instant, knowing where he was, he knew at least that he should not be there. Drowsily knowing that, he was jolted completely awake. The information, the memory and the apprehension he might need for safety or self-defense were given him in one burst. His heart swelled with the blood to nourish thought or flight; his sore muscles tightened excruciatingly in case he cared to spring away. Only his eyelids were slow, stuck together at the corners, and he rubbed them while he looked, gasping, for his gun. Seeing it, Mr. Lecky with great pain sat up. Although he was almost crippled by his stiffness he pulled the gun down from the step above.

It was the quickest, best medicine for his natural fright. Faith, said to have moved mountains, entered Mr. Lecky in force as he saw himself safely reëquipped to kill. He leaned against the rail, tottering, grunting, as each new sinew was drawn and flexed dolorously. At the same time his ears reported the perfect stillness, his eyes in rapid movement found nothing to mark but the flashlights he had dropped. He looked at his watch then, discovering, even as he remembered its uselessness, that it still showed quarter past five.

Now he was concerned about his other property: the flashlights—whether they had been damaged. Moving with a preliminary awkwardness, he saw the remains of a lens in pieces on the steps. He held the gun under his elbow and pressed the thumb switches on the others. In both cases he got, satisfied, immediate useless winks of pale yellow light. Even the broken one he might find parts for, so he attached it to his belt again, not reflecting that where these had been found were many more. Only the batteries were actually important to him, or might in time come to be.

Mr. Lecky was next aware of hunger. This tyranny astonished him. Feeding himself all his life at needlessly frequent, conventional hours, appetite had been to him hardly more than a desirable adjunct to the formalities of sitting down and waiting for food to be brought. So casual an act did not seem to have any important relation to himself as a living creature. Yesterday, fear and weariness, reliable exterminators of abstract thought, withheld the novel lesson. Today, Mr. Lecky could not miss this aspect of himself. To think that he was a contrivance which must be filled with breakfast in order to operate amused him; the trifling lightheadedness of hunger made him laugh. Food, the ham and biscuits, he had upstairs; and remembering them, he must remember his hard labor to make himself a refuge which in the end he had not used. This, too, amused him.

He began to climb, the gun grasped about the lock in one hand. He had gained the sixth floor, with two pauses only, before the impatience of his stomach reminded him that he need not eat up frugally what he already had. Food, all his, was right here in quantities to be measured by the ton.

Putting his face toward the sixth-floor doors, a certain wariness returned to him. Mr. Lecky stopped long enough to shift his gun into a position of readiness; but, stepping through, he allowed himself to be quickly reassured. He advanced with the confidence of proprietorship into the grocery department.

By long habit he ate fruit for breakfast. Somewhere there might be fruit in its natural state, but since he saw first preserved figs in a glass jar, it seemed to him simpler to eat those. He tucked his gun under his arm again and made a moment's attempt with his thumbs to break the seal of the vacuum cap. Finding the effort futile, and having no opener to give him a little leverage under the pounds of thin air which pressed it in place, he was presently moved to try the effect of striking the slightly narrowed mouth against the counter edge.

Mr. Lecky had meant only to knock the cover off; but his sharp blow was inaccurate. The neck smashed, strewing glass splinters, syrup, and a few of the figs in a mess on counter and floor. Mr. Lecky was annoyed. Furthermore, he feared that bits of glass might have embedded themselves in the remaining fruit. Setting down his gun, he made a meticulous examination, for he believed that swallowed glass would surely kill him. Partly satisfied that he was not about to eat any, he began to pick the figs out, cautiously looking over each before thrusting it in his mouth. Once or twice the grating of the fine seeds on his teeth made him pause; but hunger urged him on. Setting down the empty bottle, he could think of nothing to fetch and eat next but a second ham.

His knife was again left upstairs, he discovered. He must use his fingers. Not meant for claws, they would not serve Mr. Lecky for them. He was reduced finally to gnawing; but since he lacked the efficient incisors of proper carnivora, and his molars were flat instead of pointed, that was not easy either. He had lost his taste for ham, now that his jaws were weary and his mouth coated with the expressed oil of pig fat. Giving up, he contented himself with biscuits and water from a drinking fountain. That would do for the moment; and done, he had occasion to think of matters after all related. He must find a lavatory.

The quest took him hastily down the side of the long floor until he discovered what he sought—a door on the far side by the stairs opposite those which he had heretofore used. Closeting himself and attaining relief, Mr. Lecky had leisure to meditate, partly at least in terms of the fittings and furnishings around him. Any permanent quarters would have to be planned to include these facilities.

35

We imagine much more fitly an artificer upon his close stool or on his wife than a great judge, reverend for his carriage and regardful for his sufficiency.

Mr. Lecky, emerging at last from his retirement, stood thoughtful, with his shotgun, considering by what means he could make habitable and fortify a lavatory.

To the problem of his defense, Mr. Lecky brought a conventional imagination. The first step would be to surround himself with a wall or barricade. This would both conceal and protect him, and halt or considerably impede any attack. Nothing would so well serve this purpose as solid pieces of furniture. The furniture department would be full of them.

Mr. Lecky went at once to consult the directory and then by the most convenient stairs to the ninth floor, his mind active on the enlargement and improvement of his idea. As he had expected, the lavatories were placed one above another from floor to floor; and, standing by the lavatory door, he marked out with his eye the lines of his projected enclosure. To form it at all he would first have to move a number of heavily upholstered chairs. Pushing one chair until it bumped another, in turn bumping another, he was able to get whole rows into slow motion.

Pieces of furniture such as he had planned to use— bureau bookcases, drop-front secretaries, cabinet desks —were not conveniently placed for the purpose. He must resign himself to moving them, toil likely to be notable when only the heavier and more substantial pieces would be the ones he wanted. Reflection brought him to reduce the scale of his plan. Five pieces to a side might be enough.

Mr. Lecky took off his coat, dropped it in a chair

and laid his gun on it. That much less encumbered, he walked down among the beds. Here he picked out a cot furnished not only with springs, but with a sample mattress. Pulling it from its position, controlling its persistent side-movements, he got it easily enough roundabout through the wider aisles until it stood close to his lavatory door. Immediately he left it, and the chair where lay his coat under the gun, to select the pieces for his fort walls.

Moving the desks was hard work and it did not take Mr. Lecky long to decide that a semicircle would be a better shape for his fort than a square. It would spare him three or four trips, and if he were glad to escape extra exertion, he also shrank from prolonging in any way the noise he had to make. His heavy pieces in progress destroyed the silence with a rumbling scrape and a squeak. Some of them made sounds not impossible for a human throat to form. Some others seemed to simulate dragging footsteps. All of them, crossing certain, probably hollow, parts of the floor, made a noise like muttering thunder or far-off explosions.

At first completely occupied, and content as every man occupied completely is, Mr. Lecky, thinking how far this bang and rumble must carry, grew less content. He broke off his work frequently, restoring the silence to listen. He looked often at the stair doors near—too near—his incomplete fort. The doors hung closed and motionless. Through their panes of glass, face-high, nothing watched him; but, just as the next noise he made might be covering some sound, the instant after he looked away some countenance might rise to the empty square of glass. Like recurring cold on his sweaty face, the bad feeling that he was perhaps no longer alone kept coming and going slowly. Hesitating, his hands against the desk he had been pushing. Mr. Lecky was unable to support this doubt. He moved suddenly, ferociously agile, bounding toward the chair with his coat and gun.

The gun was still good tonic. Compact, hard, and real, it gave him a reassurance born of touch; his nerves steadied to the solid smooth stock and the long perfect steel barrel. There had been no sound when he moved; there was none now while he held the gun; and then, gradually, the sense of being secretly watched grew less and ceased. Mr. Lecky went back to his work. He took his gun with him this time, resolved not to be so far from it again; but his confidence had returned. His conscious mind believed or wished to believe that what had been no more than vaguely felt, and now was felt no more, must never have existed outside his imagination. Unconsciously, since he wanted the gun with him, notwithstanding, he could not have been blind to the other chance—a different, perhaps dreadful, good reason for feeling alone, unwatched again.

Laid on top of whatever piece engaged him, the gun went back and forth with Mr. Lecky, and so he finished his task. Leaving the last desk at an angle, he stepped into the shadows of his fort, climbed onto the table with which he had provided himself and looked over his strange rampart. He stood for some time, his elbows on a cabinet top, looking in silence. After a while he noticed that he was again hungry, and, judging it to be noon, got down. This time it would be easier to go to the eighth floor and bring up the provisions he had put there last night. He could eat, rest a little, and then move the arms and ammunition. Afterwards he must get rope to bind the pieces of his barricade into position.

When he had entered the eighth floor and crossed it, Mr. Lecky was not greatly impressed, except by their disadvantages, to see the measures he had taken for his security yesterday. He recovered his ham, beside which he saw the knife he had that morning needed. Sawing off a chunk of meat and taking a handful of biscuits, he ate both standing, anxious to complete his work.

Four guns made load enough to climb with. As for the ammunition, a knapsack or pack basket, both available among the outing equipment, would enable him to transport considerable quantities at a time. Moving to where the pitched tents stood on their platforms and mats of artificial grass, Mr. Lecky found what he wanted.

When he had made four trips, heavily laden, he rested again, ate another slice of ham, and retired to his lavatory to drink from a faucet. Refreshed, he could now consider today's trip into the store.

The pack basket on his back, the shotgun, his left hand closed over the breech and lock plates, swinging muzzle-first at his side, Mr. Lecky descended the stairs not without caution. It was, however, the caution of a man who guards prudently against the disadvantage of surprise, not that of one who expects an encounter to cost him his life.

This was well enough in the stair shaft full of diluted afternoon sunlight; but the vast main floor, so high, so open, was already shadowed. The mouths of the basement stairways seemed to be emitting a little of the abundance of darkness below. The silent sunless air was tinged with a chill gloom through which the spaced great pillars closed up in perspective. From Mr. Lecky's point of entrance, they fell into line across the floor. As Mr. Lecky advanced, they changed first into confusion,

39

then, at a certain point, into new lines drawn diagonally from corner to corner. When he reached the head of the stairs near the silverware department, they had moved again. In new departure, they were aligned from end to end.

This ordinary phenomenon of perspective was given extravagant attention, for Mr. Lecky found himself absorbed, in a way, stupefied, by the mighty effort his reason was making to keep him from being afraid. His tongue busied itself constantly with his dry lips. He breathed deeply, pushing air to the bottom of his lungs. He looked about him tentatively, up and down, once or twice sharply over his shoulder, but to no purpose. He saw and questioned details—the intricate metal nipples of a sprinkler system for fire control at regular intervals on the high ceiling; down the aisles and counters, the department numbers, the small glass and bronze signs naming the goods sold under them. He could see the silverware behind the glass of its counter fronts; he looked searchingly at the small empty information booth, down at the floor, up at the pillars. Some had the gratings of ventilators set in them. To one by the stairs was affixed the round gong, the perforated, square magnet and coil box of a big electric bell.

Mr. Lecky could not be overlooking anything, and all things were in order, and none of them needed his attention; but he found himself yawning—a spasmodic, involuntary gulp-in of the tasteless air which had nothing to do with drowsiness. Powerless to account for or to control this deep apprehension, he no longer wanted to enter the basement, or even to remain here near the stairs. Foreboding oppressed him; yet, yawning again, shaking himself a little, he looked about, not ready to be driven away, reviewing futilely the high sprinkler valves, the ventilating grills, the information booth, the silver in the counters, the big electric bell on the pillar.

Rope, he remembered, was what he had come for. He needed it to bind together his fort upstairs. There might not be any rope in the basement, and with a sort of joy, he thought how well, how much better, leather belts would be. These he could probably find on this floor, and knowing that it was no longer necessary to go downstairs, he began to wonder if he ought not to go a little way down, flash a light around and show himself that nothing was there.

Walking over and leaning across the counter whose sliding back he had last night left open, Mr. Lecky picked out one of the long-shafted torches, tried the switch with his thumb. He laid it beside his gun. He freed his shoulders from the packstraps and set the basket down. Taking his weapon in his right hand and the light in his left, he went directly to the wide stair entrance. Snapping on the light, he pointed it to strike straight and far in front of him over the descending rails and onto the open counters of the basement.

It gave him, as such play of light and shadow can, an instant's bad shock, for he thought he saw something crouched or lying on the basement floor at the foot of the stairs. The shaft of light leaped, and showed him the great variety of shadows and the mistakes he could make about him; but he was on the halfway landing, and he stopped, half satisfied, and that was enough. Turning the shaft of light in an aimless wide circle, he turned, too.

He was shaking now. The instant's halt released his joints and muscles, making him shake freely. The trembling paralyzed him. Attempting to get his body again under his direction, it seemed to resist, meaning never to serve him, never to let him get up. Then, at once, it yielded; the muscles drew, the joints articulated.

His shoes, lifting with a scrape from step to step, seemed to Mr. Lecky to echo inordinately. It was a double sound, not unlike someone following him. The insistent, the insane realness of this impression was hard to bear, and yet Mr. Lecky had no faith in it. Since he had not, courage, or his feeble assertion of courage, forbade him to perform the two natural acts—turning to see or hurrying.

At the top he faced about, jerking stiffly, and saw the staircase empty. In the relaxation of his nerves— some tense still, some eased, and so himself figuratively awry—he was exhilarated with the demonstration of such a triumph over nothing. He could even walk arrogantly through the counters searching for belts. Let anyone beware; Mr. Lecky was coming.

Finding them, he counted out the number he would need and returned. There remained nothing for Mr. Lecky to do but collect as many lanterns as he could. When he had loaded the basket, he squatted, got his arms through the straps and came erect, the pack falling into place. He departed then, pushing his way through the stair-shaft doors. His load was not light and he had a long way to go.

Resting, as he did six separate times, Mr. Lecky occupied himself with the thought of further things he might use and could get tomorrow. The measure was in a way defensive. With dusk gathering even in the stair shaft, he was suffering again that illusion of the double sound. An echo, properly his, confused itself with some blurred undertone, as of parallel movement, stopping when he stopped, moving when he moved again. On the fifth floor the illusion was so compelling that Mr. Lecky leaned on the rail and, dragging a flashlight awkwardly out, directed its light down the central void. He saw nothing except the floor far under him, the exact lines of the invariable diagonally sinking stair rails, one below another.

At last—it was darker than dusk now and he used a light—he attained the ninth floor, made his way wearily but without trouble to his silent fort. Once inside he pulled into place the desk he had left at an angle for an entrance. The pack he let down on the narrow mattress of his cot, and he sat beside it. His confidence or relief was less than he had expected. The lights to which he was ordinarily accustomed were violent, spendthrift floods. Even as many as four of these lanterns, all on together, served chiefly to show him how heavy and jealous was the outer darkness.

FOUR

The Creature Feeding

WHEN HE HAD EATEN, Mr. Lecky lay down on his cot, though he did not expect to sleep. The four lanterns continued to shed their thin floods of light. Against the dark, this illumination set the varied, ill-matched shapes of his assembled defenses. Studying the odd wall, in spirit unquiet, Mr. Lecky was reminded of his childhood—not in any detail of actual reminiscence, but more deeply, less coherently. He seemed to recall himself, unreally small and young, in concealment under a table. A table had been fort enough, for his enemies were imaginary. He never imagined them winning.

Even at that early period, furniture would only be useful against foes which he had invented to play with. Tables could not have protected him from bears or wolves. Perhaps he had been taught, by his amused elders, a conventional fear of bears. Unassisted, he had picked up a private fear of wolves. Bears were no more than vague monsters coming at night, never distinct or well defined. But of wolves his unruly imagination

44

could produce whole lifelike packs such as those which he had somehow been led to believe pursued any sleigh venturing out, three frantic horses abreast, in perpetually snow-sunk Russia.

At a brief later stage he had entertained, fruit of the new-found ability to read, some concern about ghosts. His spectres were, however, practically people, if hideous, gaunt and pale ones. It was doubtful if he ever actually believed in them, in the sense of fearing that he might meet one. His eyesight had always been good, so it played him none of the terrifying tricks necessary to confirm a belief in the supernatural. Indeed, he could not be long in discovering that people beyond a suspicion of unbalance, or not obviously coveting the moment's arrest of attention gained them by their statements, never had experience with or knowledge of the restless dead. Slowly accepting this as evidence that no such things existed, Mr. Lecky found terrors deeper, and to him more plausible, to fill that unoccupied place —the simple sense of himself alone, and, not unassociated with it, the conception of a homicidal maniac quietly pursuing him.

The first was exemplified by chance solitude in what he had considered deep woods. No part in it was played by natural dismay which he might have felt at finding himself lost, and none by any tangible suggestion of danger. Mr. Lecky could not even remember where or when it was. Long ago, under a seamless gray sky which would probably end with snow; in an autumnal silence free from birds, unmoved by the least breath of wind, he had come to be walking at random impulse.

Leaves, yellow, tan, drifted deep and loose over the difficulties of an uneven hillside. His feet crashed and crackled in them. He was not going anywhere. He had

45

nothing in mind. It might have been this receptive vacancy of thought which let him, little by little, grow aware of a menace. The unnatural light leaf-buried ground, the low dark sky, the solitary noise of his unskilled progress—none of them was good. He began to notice that though the fall of leaves left an apparent bright openness, in reality it merely pushed to a distance the point at which the woods became as impenetrable as a wall.

He walked more and more slowly, listening, hearing nothing; looking, seeing nothing. Soon he stopped, for he was not going any farther. Standing in the deep leaves beneath trees bare and practically dead in the catalepsy of impending winter, he knew that he did not want to be here. A great evil—no more to be named than, met, to be escaped—waited fairly close. So he left. He got out of those woods onto an open road where he need not watch for anything he could not see.

About his madmen Mr. Lecky was no more certain. He knew less than the little to be learned of the causes or even of the results of madness. Yet for practical purposes one can imagine all that is necessary. As long as maniacs walk like men, you must come close to them to penetrate so excellent a disguise. Once close, you have joined the true werewolf.

Pick for your companion a manic-depressive, afflicted by any of the various degrees of mania—chronic, acute, delirious. Usually more man than wolf, he will be instructive. His disorder lies in the very process of his thinking, rather than in the content of his thought. He cannot wait a minute for the satisfaction of his fleeting desires or the fulfillment of his innumerable schemes. Nor can he, for two minutes, be certain of his intention or constant in any plan or agreement. Presently you may hear his failing made manifest in the crazy concatenation of his thinking aloud, which psychiatrists call "flight of ideas." Exhausted suddenly by this riotous expense of speech and spirit, he may subside in an apathy dangerous and morose, which you will be well advised not to disturb.

Let the man you meet be, instead, a paretic. He has taken a secret departure from your world. He dwells amidst choicest, most dispendious superlatives. In his arm he has the strength to lift ten elephants. He is already two hundred years old. He is more than nine feet high; his chest is of iron, his right leg is silver, his incomparable head is one whole ruby. Husband of a thousand wives, he has begotten on them ten thousand children. Nothing is mean about him; his urine is white wine; his faeces are always soft gold. However, despite his splendor and his extraordinary attainments, he cannot successfully pronounce the words: electricity, Methodist Episcopal, organization, third cavalry brigade. Avoid them. Infuriated by your demonstration of any accomplishment not his, he may suddenly kill you.

Now choose for your friend a paranoiac, and beware of the wolf! His back is to the wall, his implacable enemies are crowding on him. He gets no rest. He finds no starting hole to hide him. Ten times oftener than the Apostle, he has been, through the violence of the unswerving malice which pursues him, in perils of waters, in perils of robbers, in perils of his own countrymen, in perils by the heathen, in perils in the city, in perils in the wilderness, in perils in the sea, in perils among false brethren, in weariness and painfulness, in watchings often, in hunger and thirst, in fastings often, in cold and nakedness. Now that, face to face with him, you simulate innocence and come within his reach, what pity can you expect? You showed him none; he will certainly not show you any.

Lighten our darkness, we beseech thee, O Lord; and by thy great mercy defend us from all the perils and dangers of this night; for the love of thy only Son, our Saviour, Jesus Christ. Amen.

Mr. Lecky's maniacs lay in wait to slash a man's head half off, to perform some erotic atrocity of disembowelment on a woman. Here, they fed thoughtlessly on human flesh; there, wishing to play with him, they plucked the mangled Tybalt from his shroud. The beastly cunning of their approach, the fantastic capriciousness of their intention could not be very well met or provided for. In his makeshift fort everywhere encircled by darkness, Mr. Lecky did not care to meditate further on the subject.

A remedy for thought was something to read; and Mr. Lecky wished to read now, at once. His desire found him nothing but the booklet of instructions regarding the shotgun. Though this was not what he meant, he produced it, mussed, from his pocket, held its small pages up to the streams of light.

However, there was one other cure for thought. Eventually, quieting, he drowsed, neither reading words, nor fearing to be alone, nor thinking of mad men.

The dark grew thin. Shining uselessly so many hours, the batteries of the lanterns were weakened. Gray light mingled quietly with theirs. Soon they were hardly more than circles of thick, illuminated glass spilling a weak yellow radiance on the table before them.

Mr. Lecky stirred and the muzzle of the shotgun dug him in the armpit. He had laid it by him when he lay down, but much good it would have done him! Shocked to realize that he had fallen soundly asleep without planning to, he could none the less see that everything was in order. Finding himself all right, he must conclude that his danger was not acute. He might, indeed, consider it proved that he had nothing living to fear, since his fort had been all night like a beacon to prowlers and none had come. Rested and cheered, he went yawning into his lavatory.

When he came out Mr. Lecky saw the ham and biscuits, available for his breakfast, with distaste. Today he would devote to collecting food more varied. And perhaps a book, he decided, remembering his last night's desire to read. And—looking at the dying lanterns which he now hastily snapped off—he would do well to depend on candles, if he could find them, for ordinary illumination. He had already largely exhausted eight big batteries.

Hoisting the empty pack basket to his back, Mr. Lecky pushed aside the desk in the corner. He passed through the swinging doors and unhurriedly downstairs. Walking with no caution he put out a hand to swing open the doors on the sixth floor. Here again he was confronted by those square panes of glass placed to prevent the accidental collision of people coming in contrary directions. Chance, or it might be the inherited ghost of a primitive faculty of apprehension, made Mr. Lecky raise his eyes, glance through.

Mr. Lecky's shock was something like that suffered by a man walking, absorbed in other matters, on a level pavement, when he reaches, without having observed it, a step down. The staggering jolt confused Mr. Lecky. He could not, for a second, collect himself enough to draw back. As it happened, his slowness was not important, for the person he saw faced the other way. Standing by the pyramided shelves this man was clumsily intent on twisting back on its key the cover of a sardine tin. When done, he instantly dug out the contents with his fingers, thrust them, animal-like, into his concealed mouth.

Mr. Lecky did step back then, with a stunned, numb delicacy. Although he was not conscious of coming to any decision, he found himself climbing the stairs, intense thuds of his heart keeping time to a progress clearly frantic. He had reached the seventh floor—two steps at a time, from toe to toe; he was halfway to the eighth floor, before the superhuman energy of his fright was exhausted. He had to pause a moment and hold the rail. A sense of the careless folly which had let him overlook his gun joined with the spasms of so bad a shock and made him ready to weep with rage. His face was mottled. His breath burnt him.

When he could, he went on. Though his hands were so weakly inaccurate as to make it actually a convenience, he was infuriated afresh and shaken into a muffled whisper of cursing to see more carelessness—the entrance of his fort left open for anyone to enter. On the steel and polished stock of his shotgun his swollen fingers were infused with the quick vibration of his pulse beat. After a moment he was able to take up the cartridge belt sagging with shells. He drew it around his waist, let the end slip and swing, having no free hand. Brought to reason, he laid down the gun a moment while he buckled the belt in place. Under it he slid the long blade of the kitchen knife, recovered his gun.

Ready now, it was time to consider his position and procedure.

To help him in judgment, or perhaps only to alarm
him, Mr. Lecky had his first picture of the unknown
adversary. There was a wide thick back, shoulders
slightly hunched, head put down, and hand raised suddenly in the wolfing of the fish. Posed so, he had been
more like a dangerously large ape in man's clothing
than a man. Mr. Lecky began nervously to wet his lips.
It might be best to seize the first opportunity to shoot
without warning. It might not be safe to temporize. A
man of the sort he had seen would be, he was convinced,
more than a match for him in a hand-to-hand encounter. He must remember, too, that his opponent might
prove to be armed, able to return fire or even to fire
first.

Mr. Lecky waited, unable to make up his mind. To
shoot down a fellow-being, deliberately, from concealment, was an act which his habit of thought held to be
atrocious. He could not look forward to the sight of
blood—or, possibly more to be dreaded, the sound of
suffering—with composure. When he moved, it was
hesitantly. A moral squeamishness aggravated the distress of shock and fear. He felt a confusion of foreboding, lest on the one hand, for all his precaution, he be
going to his own death; on the other, lest he be setting
out to contrive another man's.

Moving this time toward the doors on the far side,
Mr. Lecky was embarking on the preliminaries of the
plan he did not wish to adopt. It would begin with an
approach under cover to a point from which he could
observe his adversary. The thought, the idea of observation, was what offered him a loophole of compromise,
a covenant to withhold final decision. Accepting it, he

saw in addition, or thought he saw, another possibility. Such are the fantasies of never-chastened human wishing that some corner of Mr. Lecky's mind could harbor a hope too sweet to be plausible, too silly to bear conscious consideration, that the prowler among the groceries might have been an hallucination. In the silence of his going downstairs he framed this small, bootless appeal. Coming to the door, he laid his face against the surface of it, brought an eye to the corner of the small window. The creature was beyond dispute still there, still at his feeding.

Mr. Lecky examined him carefully. His enemy's characteristic posture appeared to be a crouch, making his movements at once careless and furtive. Every moment or two he halted, some gesture half complete, to turn his head and peer about him. Mr. Lecky could then observe the pallor of a wide face smudged with a few days' growth of beard. Either the face had no expression, or Mr. Lecky was not close enough to see any. Except for the mouth, half open, and eyes moving in their sockets, this strange man might have been carrying on his shoulders no more than a somewhat hairy lump of bloodless and fatty meat.

If there was nothing agreeable about this appearance, there was at the same time a stupid impotence which reproached Mr. Lecky with his desperately malicious scheme. Upstairs, attempting to hit on a plan, Mr. Lecky had been dealing with a fiction. His new impression worked at once to fill him with a sense of contemptuous security. The gun, which he pushed under his arm, became less an instrument of mastery than a symbol of it. His obvious course was to step out boldly, challenge and question.

Pushing the door open with no more hesitation, Mr.

Lecky advanced directly through the long series of tables set with china and glassware. Now that the plan was discarded, he was interested to see that he would have had no difficulty in getting within easy shooting distance unobserved. His frank progress did not attract attention until, conveniently near, he said: *Stand where you are!*

The sound of human speech was startling to Mr. Lecky himself; but the effect on the person he spoke to was apparently stunning. Whatever knowledge this man might have had of Mr. Lecky's presence in the store, and whatever good reason it ought to have given him sooner or later to expect this encounter, he could not have expected it now. He stood for a moment arrested in the act of reaching for something on a table. Perhaps he felt that some efficacy lay in not looking, since thirty seconds must have elapsed before he let his hand fall. Then, appalling in his slowness, he faced about.

The mouth was still open, the eyes still shifting in the bloodless oval of the big face. He made no attempt either to speak or to flee, only raising one hand against his breast and pressing it there as though his shocked heart hurt him. Then, without special sign of conscious volition, he took a mechanical step forward, followed by another. Mr. Lecky said more sharply: *Stand still! I won't hurt you.*

That his mere appearance should so stupefy and awe ought surely to be encouraging; but, instead, the perfection of Mr. Lecky's confidence suffered a trifling impairment. He felt the uncanny prolonging of the man's understandable shock. Mr. Lecky had been waiting for relaxation, the tokens of some natural recovery in eyes and expression to indicate that what he had to say would be heard and apprehended. Viewed in the thin daylight, light enough because Mr. Lecky was now used to it, but not good, the man's face stayed simply blank. Although he did stand still when told to, that seemed to Mr. Lecky more a result of the sharpness of tone given the last words than of any grasp of their meaning. The impression was quickly confirmed. Having paused, as if to let the sound pass, the man began to move. No more than a dozen yards separated them. Alarm, immediate and instinctive, brought the gun into Mr. Lecky's hands, muzzle toward this disobedient person. Mr. Lecky said: *Stand still, or I'll shoot!*

He produced again that unreal, disturbing pause. The best explanation of it actually seemed to be that his opponent was stopping to listen. Mr. Lecky's voice reached and troubled him; he thought he heard something, which he in no way connected with the figure of Mr. Lecky. Plainly he saw Mr. Lecky and meant to find out what he was. Regardless of the gun, he was coming right up to Mr. Lecky. Just as Mr. Lecky now knew that he would, the man began to move once more in the restored silence. To stop him a noise would be required. Mr. Lecky shouted, not bothering with words. The man stopped.

It could go on indefinitely, or at least—for every pause must be a few feet nearer—until Mr. Lecky was reached. Not wanting that to happen, Mr. Lecky thoughtlessly stepped back, widening the space between them. Now that Mr. Lecky moved, his opponent moved, too. Mr. Lecky, dismayed, must realize that this was turning into a pursuit. He cried: *Listen. I don't want to hurt you. But if you come any closer . . .*

His pursuer, Mr. Lecky saw, upset—for he had just assented to the theory that a voice would bring a halt—must now have decided to ignore noises which did him no harm. Mr. Lecky took two steps back and aside, around a counter. What he was looking for, he felt rather than realized, he had finally found. The gun, a moment before so embarrassingly useless as he retreated in the open aisle, resumed its value. He leaned forward, elbows on the counter corner, brought the butt against his shoulder and slid his finger around the trigger. He shouted: *One step more!*

In his agitation he did not wait for that step. Mr. Lecky's finger contracted, encountering a second's surprising, stout resistance. He tugged harder, frightened, and instantly came an explosion.

Its violence was much greater than Mr. Lecky had expected. He closed his eyes, jerking his head away. His improperly held stock dealt his shoulder a blow like a club's. Much to the right, higher, and many diagonal yards behind his pursuer's head, an array of stemmed glassware crowning a row of shelves had gone magically to pieces in the great crash of a gun fired indoors.

Mr. Lecky was too stupefied, both by the loudness of the report and the totally unforeseen blow to his shoulder, to act further. The man he was shooting at had recoiled as though similarly dazed. Both of them stood in consternation. The intense, convulsive movement of Mr. Lecky's hands performed wholly by accident on action bar latch and sliding chamber the simple gesture of reloading. The empty red shell snapping out the side made him jump, but he guessed with high-strung clarity what it meant. He jerked the slide forward again, crammed the gun against his shoulder and, wincing as he touched the bruise it had just inflicted, said: *Have you had enough?*

Receiving no response, Mr. Lecky took a threatening step into the aisle, and immediately the man wheeled about, starting to run. Mr. Lecky clutched the gun, the barrel shaking badly. This explosion was just as shocking and infinitely more painful to his shoulder, but he did not pause. Running himself, he came into the grocery department, got his dodging quarry in view again, lifted his weapon and pulled the trigger. He had, however, neglected to eject the empty shell. Aghast, he brought himself up a moment before he understood the failure. It took an additional moment to right the matter. When he was ready, the stair doors had already swung. His target had disappeared.

First impulse was to continue the pursuit without delay, for Mr. Lecky was frightened by the unwelcome thought that nothing prevented the fugitive from running up to Mr. Lecky's fort and there arming himself for shooting of his own. Mr. Lecky gained the stair landing with a rush. The man, as he might have guessed one fleeing would, had run down instead of up. The noise of steps and stumbling was unmistakably down, perhaps no more than a flight below. Mr. Lecky threw himself against the rail, tilted his gun, and though he did not know exactly where his quarry was, fired a third shell with a thunder of echoes down the shaft.

This time his shoulder pained him so that he could no longer ignore it. Holding his gun by the warm breech, he tried to ease himself by flexing the muscles, swinging his arm. Treated this way, the pain was actually not great. It was the thought of having to fire again that made him wince. Standing quietly, he could hear the noise below an instant longer, and then silence. That meant, no doubt, entrance into some lower floor, and Mr. Lecky drew breath, the emergency for the instant ended.

Now he had time to notice, a little faint, the forgotten fact that he had not eaten anything. Turning slowly, Mr. Lecky reëntered the grocery department. He could probably eat with entire security now; but, thinking of that, he thought suddenly that sleeping securely would henceforth be impossible. Laying his gun on a small stool, he helped himself to a jar of preserved figs. Abstracted, but working more carefully, or favored by a flaw in the glass, he knocked a quarter inch of the short neck and the vacuum cap neatly off together. Thoughtful, watchful, too, he began to eat, wiping his mouth and chewing slowly. Tired into a sort of calm by his vigorous activity, it was only at this moment that he saw, with the exact certainty of a premonition strongly felt, and from the first moment of the encounter, waiting on his leisure to be recognized, that whatever else his opponent was or was not, he could hardly be altogether sane.

FIVE

The Idiot Hunt

WHEN HE HAD finished breakfast, Mr. Lecky sat down and rediscovered how to load his shotgun with fresh shells from the cartridge belt. The magazine refilled, Mr. Lecky still hesitated. This time it was not indecision. His decision was made, the issue determined. Other courses might have seemed possible before, but no longer. Between himself and a sane man, not antagonized by hostilities, some understanding or agreement might be reached. With an idiot, frightened and angry, there was only one thing to do. If Mr. Lecky did not find the idiot and settle with him before it became dark, or, at least, before, exhausted, he fell asleep, the idiot would probably find and settle with the drowsing Mr. Lecky.

Seeing this, Mr. Lecky saw, too, that he had made a serious mistake in allowing the fellow to get off. He ought to have followed, never minding breakfast, his sore shoulder, or anything else, while he still had the sound of flight to guide him. With nothing to guide him, Mr. Lecky stirred uncertainly, went out to the stairs slowly. With concentrated care and attention he began to descend them.

The ground to be covered was so vast that he must eliminate some of it, if possible, and Mr. Lecky decided that it would be safe to ignore the fifth floor. He was certain that he had heard his lunatic go farther than that. Probably farther than the fourth floor, too; but here he was less sure. It would not be wise to let himself be cut off from his base. As far as the too numerous stairways would permit, he ought to try to keep the man he hunted always below him.

Considered with such elaborate caution, the circumstances gave Mr. Lecky no reason to be sure that, while he ate, his quarry had not retraced his course by stairs out of sight and hearing. He could have gone above. He could have found and profitably ransacked Mr. Lecky's ninth-floor stronghold. Mr. Lecky did not believe that he had; and, in any event, the chance, like innumerable others, would have to be taken or he would never get forward at all.

As soon as he had entered the fourth floor, Mr. Lecky found himself in departments devoted to children's apparel, baby carriages, nursery furniture. He walked out on an open rectangle, floored with dull black linoleum. On four sides were glass show cases covering set-back shelves stacked with piles of baby clothes, and for some time he looked at them, brooding. At length he thought of a sort of plan.

The plan was for a calculated quartering of the floor, begun on a fairly direct diagonal line which would bring him to the far corner. When he reached it, he turned down along the end and walked across. From this corner he moved back, intersecting the first diagonal with a second. The plan's weakness was that his quarry had perfect liberty to move around a corner or given square of counters and so stay constantly hidden. However, by this method, Mr. Lecky would see, before he was through, practically every square foot of floor space from one angle or another. Since he half believed that the man he hunted was not here anyway, and since by no means could he manage to see every square foot of the floor simultaneously, what he did was as well-considered as anything he might have done.

None the less, the sort of success which Mr. Lecky suddenly met with must be ascribed to accident. Constantly looking about him, he came again, as his course required, into the central rectangle from which he started. As he began to cross the dark linoleum he happened to look down. His eye, arrested, discovered there, outlined very dimly in dust on the smooth surface, the faint print of a shoeless human foot.

Mr. Lecky stopped short, looked up, then all around him quickly, then down at his shoes. He was convinced, too, that no such mark had been there when last he left the place. A few minutes ago his quarry must have gone through, moving naturally in the direction the foot pointed. Given thus a pointer to the idiot's whereabouts, Mr. Lecky was at the same time given urgent proof of the idiot's to-be-expected and much-to-be-feared cunning. The man had taken off his shoes to move more quietly. Inspired, Mr. Lecky stooped and with difficulty put off his own. Drawing the laces of one under his cartridge belt, he knotted them to the laces of the other, pushed the suspended shoes around on his hip, out of the way.

Determining the line of the indicated direction, Mr. Lecky moved at once, tiptoeing with alacrity. He passed between the counters at the corner, very carefully approached the outer edge, and, crouching, peered down the adjoining aisle. The simplicity of it, the complete success of the maneuver, seemed too good to be true. He saw that while his plan of search had apparently been grasped and his movements in carrying it out slyly foreseen, the print on the floor and Mr. Lecky's wise use of it had not been expected or provided for. At roughly thirty yards, back to Mr. Lecky, the big form of the man he sought was squatting. He was waiting patiently to see, from his own angle, Mr. Lecky cross the open space.

With his quarry in full sight, and so utterly unsuspecting, Mr. Lecky managed to be rid of qualms. Not that he was calm; but his unsteadiness came from an excess of jubilation. He put his elbows stealthily on the counter, holding his breath while he aligned the gun as firmly and exactly as he could to bear on the middle of this quite large target. Taking the greatest pains not to move the muzzle or shake the barrel, he crooked his index finger, drawing hard on the trigger.

This report, unheralded, purposeful and vehement, whacked out like the crack of doom. The recoil pad, better and more closely held this time, did take the sharpness off the stock's recoil, but Mr. Lecky's shoulder was tender enough to make him grunt. As for the man shot at, who could doubt that he was hit? The squatting figure, motionless an instant, gave a frightful scream. Immediately bounding, as though the impact impelled him forward, he ran, and howled again. The unhampered frenzy with which his quarry moved dismayed Mr. Lecky, but not so much as those two shocking cries. Perhaps they were fright only, for the movement seemed to show that Mr. Lecky had missed once more; and this was likely. He understood now, disgruntled, the extreme poorness of his shooting. That he could have hit fairly and yet failed to cripple did not occur to him.

Still quailing with absurd compunction, Mr. Lecky let himself lose important moments. When, recovering from the idiot's outcries, he did get into motion, running, he was brought presently to a second senseless halt. A dozen feet from where his hunted man had crouched, along the line of flight, Mr. Lecky saw something on the floor. It amounted to no more than a few wet circular spots, minutely frilled from the light impact of their fall, but it made him waver, harrowed by even this petty foretaste of his projected bloodshed. While he hesitated, he heard the dull swing of the stair doors and realized that his quarry was on the point of making a second escape. Certainly Mr. Lecky would deserve no more favors from fortune if he threw all the fruits of this one away. Hastily he followed after.

On the third floor were women's clothes. Since all sound had ceased when he gained the stair landing above, Mr. Lecky could be reasonably sure that his idiot must have gone in here. Ready to rush in, too, he stopped himself. A desperate man with no advantage but stature and physical strength might, even though demented, reason that his hope lay in coming to grips. By waiting just inside the swinging doors, he might be able to spring on his opponent, entering, with a suddenness compensating him for all handicaps.

Standing outside, well clear, Mr. Lecky could recognize the great danger he faced. He did not know and could not possibly tell which side his enemy might take. Readiness to fire and no matter how much alertness would avail him little if he guessed the wrong side, pushed the wrong half of the door, looked, for the first fatal moment, the wrong way. His idiot would be within inches of his defenseless back.

As a way out of this quandary Mr. Lecky chose finally a furtive further descent of the stairs, passage through the second floor and up other stairs, in other doors, which his enemy could have no certainty about. The time wasted, in the event that the idiot had prepared no ambush, was clearly a present from Mr. Lecky, giving that much longer to perfect a concealment. However, the whole undertaking, depending for success on the triumph of Mr. Lecky's intelligence and caution over his opponent's strength and fury, must be safeguarded from just such hazards as the closed third-floor doors might offer.

Moving with no noise, Mr. Lecky went on down. Most of the second floor was occupied by displays of blankets, bedspreads, sheets and pillow cases; but women's shoes were here also. That department, with its squares and aisles of empty chairs, gave free passage. There were no places of possible cover which Mr. Lecky need be cautious in passing. Out, and up the opposite stairway, he regained the third floor. He made a quick inspection through the glass, gave the doors an experimental push, holding his gun ready while he drew back to see what happened. Nothing happened; so he went in.

The search confronting Mr. Lecky here promised to be still more difficult than the one he had undertaken on the fourth floor. Display and sale of women's wear was more specialized, more elaborately treated and subdivided. Departments or sections imitated, in some instances, small shops, having, although roofless, walls, arched doorways, even show windows, of their own. There were, too, in almost all parts, great numbers of small fitting-rooms not unlike the eighth-floor ones which Mr. Lecky had used to make his first, never-occupied fort. Though it might be shortsighted of a fugitive to hide in places of that sort—found, no escape would remain—Mr. Lecky viewed them only in terms of their disadvantage to him, the hunter. He did not want to trap his idiot that way, at close quarters. He wanted to see him at a short but safe distance and shoot him down.

To this difficulty of so many places to hide was added another almost as great by the bad light and heavy shadows which the complicated partitioning threw in all directions. Mr. Lecky's hunt here would have every likelihood of proving futile. It could not possibly be planned. He would have to cast about at random in the constant danger of being himself surprised.

However, he might perhaps eliminate the part of the floor where he stood at the moment. An extensive array of fitting-rooms ought to be examined, but otherwise the furnishings were mainly counters for the sale of lingerie. Going by what he imagined he himself would do, Mr. Lecky decided that the idiot would never lurk here when so many places in which it would be harder to find him were close by. Trying to carry this process of putting himself in the idiot's place further, Mr. Lecky was at loss. Rushing in himself, he would have been as likely to go right as left. He took a few halfhearted steps, as though running and about to hide, but it was clearly not possible consciously to do the unconscious. He thought then of crossing to the other door and looking for more blood spots.

Going over there, he looked carefully, but he could not see anything. The man he hunted must have found some way to check his telltale bleeding. Mr. Lecky, gazing about him, examining without much hope, and so perfunctorily, possible corners and passages, took a long time to move through the display cases. Often the light was so bad that he might not have seen blood even if it were there. The floor was wood, largely covered by dull-colored thick carpeting, and dusty socks would leave no more prints. Mr. Lecky pushed his gun under his arm, stood still. After his interlude of more direct action he could hardly compel himself to take up the weary business of an extended, disorganized search.

Reluctance to proceed, mother of more inventions than necessity, now helped him a little. He did not know where the idiot was; but, at the same time, perhaps the hidden idiot did not know where Mr. Lecky was. He stepped to the edge of an aisle. It ran almost the length of the department, and at the end, perhaps a hundred yards away, he could see in the gloom the long liquid surface of a full-length mirror. Raising his gun, he fired at this, point blank.

The mirror did not come down in the cascade of metallic-backed glass which he had expected. Mr. Lecky thought at first that he must have missed; but, advancing quickly, he was soon close enough to see that the once flawless surface was clouded and starred from many points. The phenomenon so astonished him that he stood a moment bewildered. For the first time he really understood that he was not, as he foolishly thought, shooting a bullet the size of his gun's muzzle, but a cloud of pellets from a load so light that it was insignificant at that range. In this amazement he could hear, forgetful of its importance, the violent sound of the movement, which he had fired in the very hope of provoking, from his concealed quarry.

In another moment he would lose, through surprise over a stupid irrelevancy, all that his stratagem had gained him. Mr. Lecky broke into a heavy pounding rush which served him for running. He snapped over the action lever, ejecting the shell as he went, and holding the gun in both hands, tilted it carelessly toward the ceiling, firing again, snapping out another shell. He rounded a make-believe house corner representing a shop and had, to his delight, his fleeing idiot distantly in view. Without stopping or making any formal effort to take aim, he brought his gun up and fired once more.

This time Mr. Lecky shot, unafflicted by nervous preparations, with no time for complicated miscalculations, and, as occasionally happens, where he shot was exactly where he looked. The shriek of his target promptly established the rightness of this technique, and, exultant, Mr. Lecky tried it again. Now, unfortunately, he merely repeated his error upstairs in the grocery department. Ejecting the empty shell was not second nature to him; excitement precluded remembering so much. The trigger pin clicked uselessly on the already punched firing cap.

In a frenzy of chagrin Mr. Lecky fumbled for the slide. His quarry plunged into a side aisle, taking himself out of sight; but, belatedly pursuing, Mr. Lecky saw that some fresh source of blood had been tapped—much more copious. This time he stopped with deliberate consideration. His shooting was getting results, but slowly. With a trail so plain to follow, he could afford to wait a moment, fill up his magazine. To rely on the one shot left to meet who knew what emergency would be ridiculous. He laid the gun on the nearest counter and began to press shells out of the webbed loops of his belt.

The shells fitted with exasperating snugness. Mr. Lecky had to grasp the belt in one hand and from the bottom work each shell up with his thumb. The awkwardness of the operation, added to his attempted haste, and hampered, when it was, by shells already removed and still held, made him drop two while he struggled with a fourth. Each of the dropped shells rolled, perversely, in a different direction. But not so different that, stepping to snatch up one, Mr. Lecky's agitated foot could not kick the other three yards farther. With the fourth now out, he dropped that, too. Infuriated by such an ill-timed minor delay, he scrambled after them, bent, gasping, and picked up one and then the other. Turning, his unprepared eyes stunned him with a sight of the most horrible sort.

Insane or not, wounded or not, the man he hunted must have realized in the wild carelessness of desperation that his murder would be the end of this chase, that it might pay as well boldly to risk death at once as to suffer death helplessly later. He had, in incredible fact, simply doubled about the long counter. Coming without sound on his unshod feet, supporting himself against the counter with a red-streaked hand, his pale forehead and wide jowl swung forward, he meant to have Mr. Lecky's neglected gun.

Had he been quicker, less cautious perhaps, injured less, or had the fallen shells rolled as little as a foot farther, he might have succeeded. Mr. Lecky could have fainted on the breast-splitting diastole, his heart's frantic dilation. Mr. Lecky jumped. His fingers caught the stock of the shotgun, dragged it clattering over wood and glass into safety. His adversary, forestalled, had made a snatch for it, too; but it was automatic, ineffective by a yard, and he saved himself from falling only with the grip of his bloody hand. Mr. Lecky, delirious in relief and fear, retreated fast, putting space between himself and this clutching, staggering enemy. He came suddenly to his senses. He jabbed his finger through the trigger guard. He jerked the butt against his sore shoulder. He swung up the muzzle, and, the distance being no greater than ten yards, fired directly at the face of the idiot, immobile in stupor or despair, eyes doggedly fixed on him.

Although at this distance it was hardly necessary to aim, Mr. Lecky came as close as possible to missing. The load had no time to scatter in pattern, but its circumference at thirty feet was slightly greater than at the muzzle and by this fine margin Mr. Lecky hit, ploughing a hundred minute balls lightly off the side of his enemy's face and making a wound everything but fatal.

Mr. Lecky's quarry had gone down, forward on his hands and knees, but he was able with insane adroitness to crawl to his feet and flee away. He shrieked again; a sort of liquid death poured in Mr. Lecky's ear. Hoarse and formless, its high pitch broke into an airless loud whimper which went audibly with him, involuntary and purposeless.

Mr. Lecky stood still, swallowing. His mouth was awash with spittle which seemed permeated by a flavor like sucked copper and the taste of the gunpowder which he could smell. His failure to pursue was not due to prudence reminding him that his gun was entirely empty. Reason, overpowered, poleaxed, by the faculty

of sight, left him in a queasy daze, unwillingly reviewing what he had seen of that lucky shot's work. Larger,
unutterably clearer and more detailed, he beheld again,
pushing a damp hand uncertainly against his own face,
the magic pulping of that wide cheek and jaw—skin
and flesh in sudden shreds and tatters, no time yet even
to be bloody. Down from the comminuted orbit hung
the bedraggled eyeball. Half a face was entirely destroyed.

Mr. Lecky watched this image crowding on him in
monstrous anamorphosis. The butt end of his gun hit
the floor, but he held it swinging, and held the counter
edge with his other hand. Convulsed and choking, he
vomited between them on the floor.

*. . . However, the toilet of the wound should be
made for the purpose of relieving it of all kinds of
débris (broken teeth, fragments deprived of periosteum,
shreds of soft tissue) and above all to forestall secondary
hemorrhage. The latter, in fact, results most often from
the presence of traumatizing splinters, and it is gen-
erally the lingual artery that is torn by them in the
floor of the mouth. To practice this toilet no sort of
anesthesia, no bistoury, no curette, is needed. The fingers and a pair of forceps nearly always suffice. The free
splinters are lifted out, in places a still adherent shred
of periosteum is detached, to be left in the wound;
sometimes a cut with scissors is necessary to free a poorly
detached shred; sometimes again the pointed end of a
utilizable fragment is taken off with a rongeur. . . .*

Mr. Lecky, a clown in his unwonted rôle of hunter
(he wiped his mouth now; spat out the sour slime left
by his vomiting), was no better fitted for that of physi-

cian; yet, having done his poor best to kill, having at least succeeded in guaranteeing his own safety by maiming and half blinding his enemy, Mr. Lecky now felt that he must make haste after the idiot, bearing this time ignorant and unskilled succor.

By lacking the composure to ask what he purposed doing once he had come up with his quarry, Mr. Lecky helped himself into movement. Using the phrase common for emergencies which one is unequipped, or at first sight, unable, to meet, Mr. Lecky told himself that he must do something. Since all he could do was follow after, without thinking or troubling to bring his gun, he did that.

Probably he had heard, not noticing, the stair doors swing, for he went to them without question, not even bothering to see the blood on the floor. On the landing, in better light, the liberal confirming traces of his opponent's passage were harder to overlook. Leaning on the rail, Mr. Lecky heard the unspeakable drag and thump of a progress down. He could hear, too—though hardly able to let himself listen, his tongue contorted in his mouth as though he might block his ears from the inside—the gasping, imperfectly shaped whimper.

Mr. Lecky went down. On the landing of the second floor he got the injured man in sight and stopped again. One hand was laid distractedly to the torn face; the other, on the rail, sliding, locking with tenacity, held the idiot while he swayed, coming half around, his head against the banisters. Then, somehow recovering, he slipped and staggered a few steps more. Under Mr. Lecky's cheeks the muscles set themselves in a kind of cramp, narrowing his eyes, flaring out his nostrils, lodging his teeth in his lower lip. A nauseated revulsion made it seem impossible for him to move his feet in

70

the direction of this bleeding monster. He opened his mouth and cried: *Wait! I won't hurt you.*

The irony of such a promise from him was not lost on Mr. Lecky. Even the idiot ought not to be fool enough to accept it after suffering so terrible a sample of Mr. Lecky's good will toward him. Mr. Lecky was shaken suddenly. He felt a tremulous convulsion of the diaphragm which he did not recognize, for a moment of high hysteria, as the giggling it actually was. He shouted again: *Wait! I want to help you.*

Nothing was accomplished but an acceleration of the injured man's pace. In point of increased speed, it was negligible; but the frenzy of effort which went into it was appalling. Abruptly Mr. Lecky was able to move again, and he descended, almost running. The injured man reached the bottom barely a yard ahead of him, staggered, his hand on the post, and collapsed, half against it, half on the open flooring of the stair shaft.

Mr. Lecky sat down on the second step, his forearms resting on his knees, his hands hanging. After a while he noticed his stockingless feet, and detached the shoes from his belt, putting them slowly on. By looking a little to the left, through the thin steel balusters of the stair rail, he could see his victim huddled on the floor. The face was fortunately turned from him. Visible were only the obese mounds of sagging shoulders and inert, ungainly buttocks. Mr. Lecky needed to rest; but he sat there after he no longer needed to, for here was the end of his chase and there was nothing he could do—he did not know how to do anything.

The idiot's labored hoarse breathing made, minute after minute, a sound Mr. Lecky did not like. It might be due, he thought, agitated by it, to the position. That seemed to Mr. Lecky cramped and unnatural. Mr. Lecky got to his feet. Gingerly, with quaking, fastidious recoil, he finally made himself put his hands on the idiot to try to ease him or straighten him out. Except in so far as the gross bulk hampered him, this was not hard, for the body lay lax and inert. However, straining and tugging, Mr. Lecky restored his patient to a sort of consciousness. The idiot began faintly and slobberingly to shriek.

Mr. Lecky shrank back. He stood a moment wringing his useless hands, racking his empty brains. He thought distractedly of making a bandage of something, but he could not help seeing that the idiot's injuries were beyond such simple repair. In his anguish of inability, he could have howled himself, joining the injured man's outcries.

Mr. Lecky could not stand any more noise. That was the resolution of his difficulty, and the whole matter simplified itself. Mr. Lecky looked about him, rubbing his hands on his clothes, and one hand encountered accidentally what he was looking for. He went on his knees. Forcibly he turned the shattered face away, set his hand on the other cheek and bore down. The kitchen knife he took from his belt, and, though he ground his teeth with desperate distaste, he began, not hesitating, to cut, driving the point into the thick neck and pulling it stolidly from left to right.

The edge was sharp enough, and, though Mr. Lecky was not very neat or very quick, the operation was at length completed. There would be no more noise. Blood, surprisingly copious, widened out steadily on the floor, disgusting Mr. Lecky more than it horrified or dismayed him. He wiped the blade on the man's coat and laid it on the end of a step. Getting painfully to his feet, he looked about once more.

To bury his dead would be difficult. He could not dig. Yet his mind worked for him now with unemotional clarity. He stooped and took up one limp leg, drew the foot under his arm. Dragging hard, he bent forward, pulling the body to the doors. He went slowly, bowed with labor, down the wide cross aisle to the head of the basement stairs in the silverware department. There he breathed a moment, glancing around him, observing attentively but without trepidation, the information booth, the hanging department signs, the high ventilating grills, the big bell on the pillar. Perfect quiet of desertion lay over everything.

Using his foot, Mr. Lecky pushed his load off the top step. It rolled heavily, rested halfway to the landing. This did not satisfy Mr. Lecky, for it could be seen from the top. He went down and pushed it farther. Grunting and shoving, he got it across the landing and sent it tumbling to the bottom, where it brought up, supported against the stair rail.

SIX

The Fruits of Toil

Mr. LECKY REASONED that
his gunfire often repeated, announcing his arrival in
floor after floor, would have brought out other lurking
foes, had any been there. Thus he rid himself of the dis-
trust which might make him attempt some impossible
vigil after this exhausting day. Of other concerns he had
none. Finally reaching his fort, he was in no way con-
scious-stricken to know himself a murderer, and to see in
the last light, dry on his hands, the dirty stain of blood.
Washing in the lavatory, his hands did not incarnadine
more than a minute's flow of water. Here, where no
one could take him, force out his guilt, and kill him for
it, Mr. Lecky felt no more remorse than Cain, his proto-
type. He dried his hands on the end of a roll of coarse
paper meant for towels. He went out and fumbled in
the dark shadows until he found his torches. Though
they were much less convenient than the largely used-
up lanterns, they would stand on their ends if he did
not shake the table.

These strong shafts of light struck the white ceiling and were reflected back. Mr. Lecky could see well enough to eat. He brought his chair over and sat down gratefully while he consumed, but with appetite now, the ham and biscuits which he had disdained in the morning. Even the fact that he was using to cut his ham the knife which had cut a human throat did not disturb him. He had taken care to see that the blade was wiped clean. Sunk in the content of rest after labor, he thought again of the candles he had meant to get, of the book to read, but his failure to have them was no inconvenience. He would not need light long; nor did he wish to read tonight.

Stretching on his cot, the darkness soothed Mr. Lecky. He put a flashlight where he could reach it, but when his mind, fussing in normal protest against so much bodily ease, recalled to him that he had left his gun down on the third floor, he shrugged a little, not enough disturbed to act, and giving it no further heed, very soon slept.

It was day when Mr. Lecky awoke. He opened his eyes without starting; he did not experience the usual falling qualm of apprehension. He stirred, finding himself stiff from yesterday's exertions. His right shoulder was, in fact, extremely sore. Sitting up, he rubbed it tenderly; yet the pain it caused him was unessential, mere surface twinges. Fundamentally he felt well and alert, confident in his new security. He was pleasantly aware that today he would be free to make a thorough examination of the riches of the extraordinary domain now his. Never in his life having been able to own or enjoy quite enough of anything which cost more than the most trifling sum of money, the thought that now he had everything excited him. He got promptly to his feet and went into his lavatory.

Returning, he swung on his pack basket, walked out, cheerfully, and downstairs to the grocery department and as good a breakfast as he could find. Eating it, he gave up his first idea, which had been to fill the basket with food. That was a waste of energy. Since no one could prevent or interrupt him, it would be easy to come down here for meals. Eating, he could reflect, too, on the great benefit which any means of cooking would be to his diet. Somewhere, surely, he might find tinned fuel, for use in circumstances like his.

Candles (he still had in mind yesterday's list of things he needed) were to be found on the seventh floor. Mr. Lecky walked leisurely up there after breakfast. Discovering them in great quantities, drawers full of many colored ones in many shapes and sizes, he filled his basket with the largest—tapers perhaps two inches in diameter, wrapped in tissue paper. Each should burn brightly for a long while. He carried up the load and deposited it on the table in his fort.

This took only a little while, but the tinned fuel he had thought of would undoubtedly be in the basement with hardware and household supplies. Mr. Lecky hesitated a moment, remembering what else was there, but his frown was purely practical. He was not satisfied with his disposal of the dead man. Soon the body, beginning to rot, would stink. A better idea would have been to take it and shut it up in some closet or lavatory; yet, on the whole, it might not matter a great deal. Mr. Lecky would spend most of his time many flights upstairs, and the putrefaction could hardly contaminate more than the immediately surrounding atmosphere. If he got today what he needed down there, Mr. Lecky would not have to know anything about it.

Acting quickly, as though minutes might make a difference in whether or not he were greeted below by some revolting stench, Mr. Lecky pushed a flashlight through his belt, resumed his basket, and reaching for it, remembered about his gun. He could stop on the third floor and get it—but on the way up, he decided, for there was no reason to carry it around with him. On the way up, too, he could stop and take a book to read from the department on the main floor.

The task of looking, with the spot of a flashlight, through the dark immensities of the basement for a few small cans, which Mr. Lecky was, at best, only presuming were there, had natural difficulties. In the stair shaft, walking downstairs in the strong white light of the fused glass, a faint shadow before him, the basket on his back squeaking casually with each step, he had anticipated no particular difficulty; but, arrived on the main floor, he saw with disapproval the wide dark stain on the stair-shaft pavement, the dried smears and spots of a track passing through the doors. He turned at once, walked back to stairs as far as possible from those in the silverware department.

Mr. Lecky went down without reluctance; but in the confusing darkness he found it hard to be easy and unhurried, for he saw that this search might take hours. He passed quickly through a corner where his moving light fell over kitchen tables and enameled cabinets. Nor did he want complicated frames for drying laundry in a small space, little stands to aid in the cleaning of shoes, or ranks of folding stepladders. Inquiringly shifted, his light showed him next, gardening utensils, coiled lengths of rubber hose, piled sacks of chem-

77

ical fertilizer. Some of the counters were cut into bin-fuls of different dry bulbs, bags of grass seed, small paper envelopes containing seeds of the vegetables and flowers pictured in color on them. These were of no use to Mr. Lecky.

Traveling on, the shaft of his light reached now a great, dully shining oblong, and he stopped, surprised. Then, through the glass sides, he saw bright shapes of fish wheel in schools down the opaque water, startled by the illumination. Coming at last, and so suddenly, on life like his own, Mr. Lecky moved closer. The fixed flood of his light enveloped these small fish dimly, glowed back on him. They came sliding, drifting, mouths in motion, gills rippling, up the light, against the glass. Their senseless round eyes stared at Mr. Lecky. Idling with great grace, the extravagant prod-ucts of selective breeding—fringetails, Korean, calico —passed, swayed about, came languidly back. Moving faster, stub-finned, crop-tailed danios from the Mala-bar coast appeared, hovered, taking the light on their fat flanks, now spotted, now iridescent pearl or opal.

Seeing so many of them, so eager and attentive, Mr. Lecky felt an unexpected compunction. He was their only proprietor; and soon, trapped unnaturally here in the big tank, they would starve to death. His light went back to a counter he had just passed, showing him again the half-noticed packages—food for birds and pet animals, food, too, for fish. Returning to the tank, his light found many of the fish still waiting, the rest rush-ing back. He went and took a package, tore the top off, and poured the contents onto the rectangle of open water. It would perhaps postpone the time when, hav-ing eaten each other, the sick remainder must die anyway.

Mr. Lecky dropped the empty package. In the dark a curious low sound reached him from beyond the tank. He jumped about, his light going with him. There was silence, and then suddenly, bringing them to his attention, from a long line of hanging bird cages, a chirping, a brush of feathers and flap of stretched wings. Uncertainly followed a few thin bursts of song, as though Mr. Lecky's light had persuaded some of the birds that a new day was dawning. Accepting this added responsibility, Mr. Lecky went over and, passing down the line, found and opened one after another the cage doors. No birds came out, but hunger might eventually make them come out. Being able to fly at will, they could perhaps find food among the seeds.

Impatient at the time he had wasted on these merciful acts, Mr. Lecky moved on into a section full of bathroom fixtures: racks, soap dishes, cabinets on the wall whose mirrors turned back at him the bright circle of his light and a glimpse of his own pale face behind. Now he was approaching the front, and he halted, for after all, he had been here before. The stairs were over there, and at the foot of them lay the carcass of his idiot. Mr. Lecky shot his light that way in a hasty, unplanned movement. The stairs jumped out of the dark just where he had imagined they would be; but they were too distant for any exact scrutiny. Turning sharply, Mr. Lecky crossed the whole width of the floor.

Paints and varnishes piled up in orderly labeled rows on shelves along the side. Near here, if anywhere, Mr. Lecky was inspired to realize, would be his tinned fuel; and, as he walked, paint finally gave way to polishes, waxes and cleaning fluids. Just beyond them, he beheld, triumphant, what he wanted. Shrugging off his pack basket, shifting the flashlight from hand to hand, he took down the cans. On the counter stood a metal frame with two of the cans in position beneath it, showing how it would serve as a flimsy, improvised stove. He seized that, too, folding the legs under and thrusting it in his basket.

Next, he should carefully consider whether he wanted anything else down here; but if he did want anything, his mind, obsessed abruptly with the desire to get up into the light, would not think of it for him. Shouldering his basket, he started off for the stairs.

Mr. Lecky had proceeded quickly for several moments before he drew up, shocked. A few more steps and he might have stumbled on his idiot, for the stairs he had been approaching were the front stairs to the silverware department, which he wished to avoid. Shaken by this unpleasant mistake, he re-directed himself, turning back down the center of the dark floor. Certainly he did not want to see the corpse; the corpse could not very well want to see him.

However narrowly, the ghastly meeting had after all been avoided. Safe up in the good enough light of the main floor, Mr. Lecky's relief made him cheerful. He was now reminded of the book he had planned to get.

It was the habit of his years of security prevailing over more recent but brief experience which made Mr. Lecky so poor an observer. On his way back here, intent on his errand downstairs, he had given little attention to his surroundings. Coming up again, he was surprised to step out on the edge of a department where nothing but books was sold. Books were all around him, solidly packing the shelves on the walls, stacked in rows and tiers and mounds on every table.

Putting off his basket, Mr. Lecky began at random

to handle the books on the first table. So many of them made him doubtful, for while he wanted a book, he wanted it only if he could be fairly sure that his trouble in reading it would be repaid. He examined the clean jackets; he let the new pages run past his fingers. Turning the leaves of a book, he could sometimes judge from the proportion of the broken lines of conversation to solid and unbroken paragraphs whether the work would be tedious to read. Still at loss he saw finally a volume whose paper jacket bore the arresting silhouette of a nude woman. He snapped it open, to face page after page of closely printed words without dialogue. However, the jacket picture seemed to promise a subject matter which he could read with attention. Satisfied, he pushed it into his basket, only mildly embarrassed to find himself yielding to so improper an urge. After all, there was no one here to shame him by the discovery of his low choice.

His sharp appetite suggested luncheon.

When he had eaten (he would put off attempting to prepare a warm meal for himself until evening), Mr. Lecky, in the lavatory, looked at a mirror. Unless he purposed to grow a beard he must do something about shaving; and faced with this annoyance, he wondered why not have a beard. Every day for years he had frustrated the efforts of his physical organism to provide him with one, never checking or discouraging the attempt, so it seemed certain that he could grow whiskers on his face. The novelty of the idea interested him. It might give him a more imposing appearance.

Transferring his attention from his face, already darkened by the neglected first stubble of sprouting hair on cheeks and chin, he saw that he ought to get himself new clothes. He ought to throw away these garments, worn, torn, spoiled with dust and spilled food and dried blood. There was no reason why he should not have all the clothes he wanted. More, if he chose, than he could ever use, a splendid super-abundance of garments—selected, furthermore, because he fancied them, not because they promised to wear well, be slow to show how dirty they were, and attract no attention by undue individuality or brightness.

Descending promptly to the fifth floor, Mr. Lecky entered the men's clothing department. Sliding back the wide glass doors of a case, he took out a suit. Removing the coat from the form that held it and laying the trousers on a chair, he took off his own disreputable coat and thrust an arm into the sleeve of the new one. It was a great deal too small.

Mr. Lecky noticed, however, that a cardboard oblong was sewed lightly to the cuff. On it was printed a number, plainly the price, a number which must mean size, and a number with no meaning Mr. Lecky could guess. A higher size number might be a larger garment. Pushing the door all the way back, Mr. Lecky took up the hanging sleeves, consulting the successive cards. They ran, he found, in obvious progression, increasing finally in size enough for even his inexperienced eye to note it. He took down what he judged would be more nearly right.

This coat was easy to get into. The sleeves neither stopped halfway down his forearms nor extended so far as to obstruct the use of his hands. Buttoning it, he found that the cloth drew tightly over his abdomen; but this was a difficulty he very often had even when someone assisted his selection. The slight feeling of constraint gave him a not unpleasant sense of being girded up, made more compact and efficient. Had there been anyone to say it to, Mr. Lecky might easily have said that this would do, self-consciously brusque and indifferent—perhaps the more so because the cloth, while answering the factitious requirements of the dinginess and probable durability, did not please him in the least.

Even now it would do. He might as well take it, since there need be no limit to the number he could have. Dropping it, he turned to seek his size in cabinets where the garments were higher priced and presumably better. Engaged thus, pulling out the sleeves, holding up the cards to see them and the cloth, he took down a suit from time to time, tossed it out on the floor. He was absorbed in the petty pleasure of gratifying his liberated taste. He had found his number on the sleeve of a rough tweed coat, checked brown, as nearly as the light served him, almost to the point of orange. Bringing it out, he removed his trousers, ready to pull on the trousers supplied here. Still holding the coat, he stopped then, aware by a sudden instinctive horripilation of his skin and tightening of his scalp that something surely terrible was in progress.

. . . the Egyptians after their feastings and carousings caused a great image of death to be brought in and shewed to the guests and bystanders, by one that cried aloud . . .

Mr. Lecky's realization had been delayed. It was necessary to tear his attention away from what he was doing and give it to what seemed only a minor distraction, or at most, a baseless foreboding. He stirred and roused himself, feeling the foreboding rather than hearing the sound. An instant passed, and he began to hear as well as feel. Muffled by distance, but clamorous wherever it was, and carrying far through the store below him in the stillness, an electric bell rang peal on reiterated resonant peal.

The vibration of it seemed to be left hanging on the air everywhere after it suddenly stopped and the brief persistence of this echo gave the whole ringing unreality. Conscious of himself standing just as the sound had surprised him, in graceless undergarments showing his fat and hairy legs, and the shirt hanging its loose tails below his rump, Mr. Lecky lifted his foot and began to put the trousers on. He took the coat and put that on.

Almost sure that he could not have heard any such thing, Mr. Lecky was none the less still listening. He was rewarded by soon detecting the slight steady ringing in his own ears. Strained for and studied, it became loud, as loud as a distant bell, especially when there was no bell to ring and no one to ring a bell. Mr. Lecky's spirits tried to rise a little in relief. This explanation was obviously the right one, yet, restive and curious, his thought drew away from it, traveled skipping from floor to floor down, down, and Mr. Lecky recoiled, closing his hands, able to see the high sprinkler valves, the ventilating grills, the information booth, the silver in the counters, and, on the pillar by the basement stairs, the round gong, the perforated square magnet and coil box. . . .

Mr. Lecky gave over his clothes-collecting. He left everything and walked upstairs.

Regaining the ninth floor, Mr. Lecky found himself on the far side, distant by the whole furniture-crowded department from his fort. What change had overtaken him, Mr. Lecky did not know. Never before had he entered here without a desire to put himself inside his defenses. His coming up must have been with the assumption that so he wished to do now; but he did not. His circle of furniture suggested only a pen or a prison. In the gloom of its added shadows he would have nothing to do but sit and listen.

He paused. He moved on. His feet were taking him there. He could not reason with such an urge; he could only resist it a little by going a long way. From the stair doors he passed down the side, looking in at a series of open-sided rooms where pieces picked from the scattered displays on the floor had been arranged in formal, deserted tableaux, to show them as they would look, or might best look, in apartments where people actually lived.

Mr. Lecky's reluctance to get where he was going let him glimpse, although inattentively, with impotent appreciation, the setting for lives less strait, more expensive and easier than his own had ever been. To wash and relieve his natural wants merely as a matter of course in such a bathroom as he passed now—and stopped, in spite of everything, to look at again—might epitomize Mr. Lecky's mortal hopes. The utilitarian fixtures were all of pale-yellow porcelain. Mirrors, glass doors, polished stone wainscoting, reflected what light they caught.

Perhaps he stood too long, losing his anxiety, for, not starting, but with the same previous slow realization, Mr. Lecky knew that his bell was ringing impatiently. It was a little fainter; it must, indeed, proceed from the point he had thought of far below. He turned in a sad stupor, as though he hoped to see the line of the sound's approach. Soon it stopped.

SEVEN

The Table in the Wilderness

THE IDIOT LAY downstairs in the hole Mr. Lecky had chosen for him. Mr. Lecky, upstairs, went to his fort. Arriving, he saw in the gloom and touched the things he had that morning brought there. They had lost savor now. They promised nothing. He picked up this, to set it down and take that, shaking his head from side to side. A mortal ennui, coming to live with him, made its residence by tossing out the small baggage of Mr. Lecky's plans and desires. His brain was void of purpose, airless, chill as an empty house.

Brooding, he sat still, bemused by nothing while time passed and the afternoon ended slowly. As far as he was consciously or intellectually concerned, he might have sat forever in the luxury and insentience of despair. Yet to brood, to despair, even to sit, he must be fed. There was no relief from this endless schedule of food; and if he could or would not think to provide himself, his belly could promote the reflexes which, without his thinking, would provide for him.

Mr. Lecky was going downstairs. Under his arm he pressed the light metal frame of his stove. He carried two cans of fuel, an electric torch, and, angling out his coat pocket, a thick candle. He had left matches in his discarded suit. Since his stomach was ready for food, he went to get matches, so that he could cook. When he had found them, he returned to the sixth floor and, still inconscient, set about his supper.

He had no pot to cook in, and no implement to open a can. The latter Mr. Lecky found. Such things he looked for in drawers, and so now he opened what drawers he saw until, unsurprised, he discovered an instrument which would take off bottle caps, rip tin, draw corks. He lit his taper then. Holding it at an angle, he let the liquefied paraffin spill on the table until there was enough to harden and hold the candle erect. By this light he cleared a space and set up his stove.

Prying the lids from the fuel cans he put them in place. The candle flame grew brighter while he did it, and he stood regarding its shaking, sharp-pointed spatula, dumbly observing the short work it made of darkness. Turning finally he glanced at the illuminated shelves encircling the pillar behind him. That they should be lined with the repetitious labels of soup tins stirred a spark of interest, a surprised appreciation. His experience resigned him unreasonably to the idea that what was convenient or to be desired would always be found far away, after irksome effort. The can opener made one, and this made two things as convenient as possible.

Twenty sorts of soup stood there, and several brands. Mr. Lecky's interest did not extend to making a choice, and the mere fact that a choice could be made reduced him, for a moment, to helplessness. Finally, spurred by the appetite to which he was indifferent, he took any one, read the printing on the parti-colored label of paper. He held the soup can like a skull; and at once he did not want it. The soup was made from celery. Mr. Lecky put it back. He stood in mild misery, harassed again by the plague of a will impotent in its restored freedom.

If the mind cannot direct, it can be cunning to protect its ease. Mr. Lecky now proposed a fantastic pact to himself. He shut his eyes. He reached again and took a can. Eyes still shut, he ripped the label from it, crumpled and threw away the paper. Now he could not tell what he had until he opened it.

He touched a struck match to the waxy surface of the substance filling a fuel tin. The heat melted it. The resulting liquid caught in a lifting swirl of insubstantial violet flame. Over this fire, on the frame of the little stove, he placed his can. With no thought of the blind and terrible force so simply and stupidly to be evoked, Mr. Lecky moved about, compelling himself to think of other things to fetch for his meal. At intervals he stood and watched, innocently hoping that his can was getting hotter. Finally he put out a finger to see if it were hot. He did not touch it, for he did not have to. Put near, his finger tips felt the radiations of sheet steel under the titanic stress of steam. The microscopic structure, its cohesion jeopardized, was shaking like jelly. Mr. Lecky bent down to blow out the colored flame.

Swirling, it flattened away before his breath, but it had a tenacity of its own and Mr. Lecky straightened up, defeated. He would slide the cover over the fiery mouth, he decided, and extinguish it that way. Now, he reached for the cover, and chance was surely his friend

again. Had his face been down there, to meet the out-
rageous explosion halfway, he might have got it all.
As it was, only a little of the scalding mess of vegetables,
flying fanwise, spattered his neck and the side of his
head.

Mr. Lecky gasped in anguish multiple and breath-
taking. He pawed away the vegetable débris, clinging
venomous with its saturating steam, and burned his fingers. He took a few blind steps. He corrected himself,
thinking of cold water. He stumbled against a table
in the shadows and precipitated an avalanche of the
small articles piled there. He could not find the lavatory door, but the porcelain bowl of the drinking fountain came to his eye. He clutched at it, shot up its jet
of water, swung his stinging cheek and neck back and
forth across this minute stream.

The cool wetness did afford relief—enough to stay
the immediate thoughtless impulse of anguish, and so
to allow Mr. Lecky to remember that water would only
end by augmenting the smart. Some salve or ointment,
oiling the scalded skin and shutting out the air was what
he needed. Any such thing would be found far below
among drugs and what were called toilet articles on
the main floor.

Five minutes ago Mr. Lecky would not have gone anywhere, could not have brought himself to seek a hundred yards for anything. He was enlivened now. Void
then of desire, he was now filled up by pain, given the
most engrossing kind of absorption. Neither darkness nor distance impressed him. He held his hand
against his throbbing neck, returning to the scene of
his small disaster with brisk, purposeful haste. He took
his flashlight from the table. A sharp smell of burnt
vegetables came to him, but the flame in the fuel tin

had been smothered. Leaving only the solitary candle burning, he went, the shaft of light hopping along the floor in front of him, to the stair doors.

On this business or that, Mr. Lecky had traversed before most of the front sections of the main floor; so he knew where to go to find what he wanted. Even if he had not known, he might have been guided as he passed directly toward the back by the slow suffusing of the air with one general odor of many mixed scents—soap and perfumes. The beam of his light twitched up, swinging through the middle air. It picked out a hanging oblong of glass on which gold letters spelled PROPRIETARY MEDICINES.

Mr. Lecky soon stepped behind a counter and began to open the deep lower drawers, sending his light over piles of boxed tubes of tooth pastes, shaving creams, cold creams, ointments, until he found one of the last whose name was familiar to him. Tearing the cardboard, unscrewing the small cap, he squeezed out some of the contents, smeared it with confidence over his neck and face. Looking up, he saw on the shelves bottles of what he believed to be a cooling and healing extract. He could apply this in the morning and so complete his cure.

Mr. Lecky succeeded in working the large bottle into his coat pocket. Shifting his light inquiringly, he wondered if there were other things he might want or could use to be found here.

Moving on, while he wondered, the dark through which Mr. Lecky's light cut grew more beautiful with scents. Particles of solid matter so minute, gases so subtle, that they filtered through stopping and sealing, hung on the unstirred air. Drawn in with Mr. Lecky's

90

breath came impalpable dews cooked out of disintegrating coal. Distilled, chemically split and reformed, they ended in flawless simulation of the aromas of gums, the scent of woods and the world's flowers. The chemists who made them could do more than that. Loose on the gloom were perfumes of flowers which might possibly have bloomed but never had, and the strong-smelling saps of trees either lost or not yet evolved.

Mixed in the mucus of the pituitary membrane, these volatile essences meant more than synthetic chemistry to Mr. Lecky. Their microscopic slime coated the bushed-out ends of the olfactory nerve; their presence was signaled to the anterior of the brain's temporal lobe. At once, thought waited on them, tossing down from the great storehouse of old images, neglected ideas—sandalwood and roses, musk and lavender. Mr. Lecky stood still, wrung by pangs as insistent and unanswerable as hunger. He was prodded by the unrest of things desired, not had; the surfeit of things had, not desired. More than anything he could see, or words, or sounds, these odors made him stupidly aware of the past. Unable to remember it, whence he was, or where he had previously been, all that was sweet, impermanent and gone came back not spoiled by too much truth or exact memory. Volatile as the perfumes, the past stirred him with longing for what was not—the only beloved beauty which you will have to see but which you may not keep.

Mr. Lecky's beam of light went through glass top and side of a counter, displayed bottles of colored liquid—straw, amber, topaz—threw shadows behind their diverse shapes. He had no use for perfume. All the distraction, all the sense of loss and implausible sweetness which he felt was in memory of women.

Behind the counter, Mr. Lecky, curious, took out bottles, sniffed them, examined their elaborately varied forms—transparent squares, triangles, cones, flattened ovals. Some were opaque, jet or blue, rough with embedded metals in intricate design. This great and needless decoration of the flasks which contained it was one strange way to express the inexpressible. Another way was tried in the names put on the bottles. Here words ran the suggestive or symbolic gamut of idealized passion, or festive night, of desired caresses, or of abstractions of the painful allure yet farther fetched. Not even in the hopeful, miracle-craving fancy of those who used the perfumes could a bottle of liquid have any actual magic. Since the buyers at the counters must be human beings, nine of every ten were beyond this or other help. Women, young, but unlovely and unloved, women, whatever they had been, now at the end of it and ruined by years or thickened to caricature by fat, ought to be the ones called to mind by perfume. But they were not. Mr. Lecky held the bottle in his hand a long while, aware of the tenth woman.

Finally he put it down. Picking up his flashlight and turning, he had moved perhaps three steps when, sharp and clear, plainly at the point from which he had first imagined it, broke out the resonant, now nearby, clamor of the bell.

Mr. Lecky jerked his chin. He raised his hands, pressing the palms over his ears, dropped them, moving his head again as though he hoped this sound could be shaken out like loose water. The sharp pealing stopped then, but of itself. He had not done it by either futile measure. Knowing this, his mind was frenzied with his desire for explanation. If, to pay its stubborn poor service, he beat his head with his fists, the protest must be ineffective; Xerxes whipped the sea to better purpose. Inappeasable fury to know mounted the little higher it could; the great tempest of his re-aroused despair tossed him. It was no longer mental only. He struck about him with his hands, hitting the air, but that did not help. Running, he dashed the bottles from the counter behind. They broke audibly on the floor, spilling their perfume in pools. At last, in final extravagant spasm, he hurled his flashlight away. Its shaft turned, undirected, still shining an instant in the air. It struck then, went out instantly, leaving him in total darkness.

Mr. Lecky's hand found the counter edge. Moving, his feet broke again the glass of broken bottles. He stood still, and the strong smell of synthetic flowers surcharged the darkness. A quiet slowly followed on the whirlwind. Since everything had failed—close thought, fury, his folly of destruction—he must now make failure what he wanted. Since he could not find the cause, it was time to submit, content himself with knowing the result.

Mr. Lecky, giving in, no longer insisting on any explanation, had been sorely tried, but contrast would enhance his reward. Fear could not recrudesce in him; terror could spur him no further. Fear's many inventions—solitude, darkness, the chance of enemies prowling in the flesh with weapons to kill him, the chance of enemies disembodied, walking his own mind, with the means to drive him mad—no longer had weight with him. They had not injured or killed him yet. He was alive. When he moved, it was with resignation. He did not walk cautiously, for darkness was nothing to him. He did not listen for enemies. If he met any it would be time enough to worry about them. He did not mind being alone; to live, his body was sufficient to itself. What he could not see or explain would have to go its way, as he now went his.

The climb upstairs was long, but, keeping close to the stair rail, he had no difficulty. On the sixth floor his candle was still burning, a small calm light over the débris of the little explosion. Taking the candle in his hand, Mr. Lecky climbed up to his bed. Yawning, he blew out the flame.

The architectural limitations of a room are the next consideration. They include its size and proportion, as well as the placement of doors and windows and fireplace. Then there is the style of the decorative treatment to be reckoned with. A fine classic moulding and smooth wall surface demand furniture that is harmonious in feeling. . . .

No two of the pieces of furniture which had gone to make up Mr. Lecky's fort precisely resembled each other. When Mr. Lecky awoke, lying on his uncomfortable cot, he could see the line of a crazy confusion against the light. Most of the cabinets were not set even or exactly straight. The table, the chair, the cot he lay on, were shoved in carelessly, not arranged.

Work was irksome to Mr. Lecky, but idleness was worse; it was insupportable. Rather than face idleness he could, at least for a while, find things to be done where there was none, and somehow impose on himself the slavery essential to happiness or mere peace. Hopefully he began to find fault with the fort which he had worked so hard to construct. Remembering his harassed inspection yesterday afternoon, it occurred to him that he could, if he chose, set up a new and better establishment in the model rooms across the floor. Without waiting to get himself any breakfast, he was impelled to go at once and see if this were feasible.

Nothing hindered Mr. Lecky's entrance into these apartments but thick velvet cords hooked into rings. He moved down the row, counting to fourteen. All of them were his and all the good and interesting things in them awaited his disposal. There were, for instance, beds of obvious comfort and actual luxuriousness. Mr. Lecky unhooked and let fall a velvet cord. He was recently enough risen from his narrow cot to feel satisfaction at such an improvement. He walked soundless on a carpet taupe-colored and of great thickness. A canopy overhung the bed-head with the same flowered percale which hid all but the edges of the woodwork and formed a spread as well. Sitting on the edge of the bed, Mr. Lecky regarded, less pleased, the walls in old white. They were painted preciously in an Italian manner two centuries old to imitate plaster moulding. Pink had been used. Carrying the scheme to deeper tones, a slipper chair in cherry-colored satin, an armchair considerably curved with white painted wood and flowered chintz; a side chair, at the false window, in red and white stripes had been added.

Still testing the bed, Mr. Lecky's first objection grew less. It was founded mainly on his idea of what some imaginary person, whose scorn he feared, might think of him, if such were shown to be the room in which he lived. Left to himself, Mr. Lecky found the shape of a chair, the color of upholstery, a small matter. Wellfitted, strongly fashioned joints, solid wood, thick padding firmly attached, were the real virtues. There was an element which he considered feminine in this room, and he arose, doubtful, resolving to get himself break-fast before he made any decision.

Downstairs, feeding from the edge of the counter, he had the litter of previous meals in sight. More work suggested itself to him. Henceforth he could eat in a real dining-room, with a table and chairs to sit on; and this greater convenience ought to compensate him for the trouble of carrying up food. He could set about that as soon as his bedroom was definitely selected and such things as he wanted moved over from his fort.

A second, more thorough investigation showed Mr. Lecky that he might do well to like the bedroom in pink and old white and cherry, the abundant flowering percale. Orchid and pale green and some shades of yellow decorated a room which he considered undoubtedly pretty, but less suitable still. Another supplied twin beds, but he could after all only use one bed.

Returning, thus resolved, to his fort, he set about filling his pack basket once more. He would want his candles and the flashlights, his book. He had also that bottle of witch-hazel extract and the tube of ointment. He had not so much as noticed his burns this morning, but he might as well take his medicines. The witch-hazel, he understood, if needed for no other purpose, could be drunk, producing an agreeable effect. The idea was an irregular and improper one. Drinking it, he was sure, would not be good for him; but his facile curiosity led him to unscrew the cap and taste the contents cautiously. He did not like the flavor, but report was correct. It was drinkable—not too revolting.

Looking now in his lavatory, to see if he had left anything there, he was reminded of the sumptuous bath-room he had looked at yesterday. Distributing the things from his load where they would be handy in the pink room, he turned and went to examine this fine place. As he had more than half foreseen, he found that it was not real. He twitched the faucets one after another, but no water came out their golden mouths. Leaving, disgruntled, he looked around for a washroom to replace the distant one which he had fortified.

Mr. Lecky's discovery that none was nearer displeased him, expecting, as he did now, every comfort; but since the need to have protected communication with it was presumably over, he could manage. He stepped into a dining-room furnished in heavy carved oak and red plush. Sitting in the monumental chair at the table's head, he rested while he planned further.

This was the place in which he would like to eat; so a supply of food enough for several meals ought to be brought up here. He would need, too, dishes and eating utensils. Heretofore he had got on well enough without them, but he did not mean to eat so informally in this fine and spacious setting. To the disagreeable problem, immediately presented, of washing the things he used he had a simple solution. He could throw soiled dishes away and help himself to clean ones from the great stocks on display on the sixth floor.

Up and down stairs Mr. Lecky passed, bearing his pack basket. To store his food he made convenient use of the large double-doored cabinet against the wall. The top of an oak chest standing under the simulated casement window would serve him for a kitchen. He included the stove and fuel tins in his next load. In his hands he carried up several plates and a glass. He was making progress, but he still had no implements to eat with, aside from his so variously used kitchen knife, and nothing to cook in. Since he wanted work to occupy

97

him, he should be glad, for he knew how much work getting those things would be.

Descending the endless stairs for the sixth time, Mr. Lecky thought of all the goods those closed doors hid. Fantastic was the discouragement it caused him. Aware of such variety and great quantity, Mr. Lecky saw the danger of forgetting or never even imagining things which, discovered, he would want. Everlastingly midway between two equal errors, to which could he cleave? To have time for everything, one must make haste. To gain access to everything, one must be patient.

Moreover, hasty, or patient as Job, with what great labor would Mr. Lecky carry up on his back all he got! Making, as he was every moment, the climb back longer, giving, as he did with each step down, consent to toil more and more severe, he could anticipate vaguely and abhor another possibility. Curious and insubstantial as his fearing not to find what he could not think of, was his resentment of a perhaps coming time when he might, in revolt against the inanity of exertion, live meanly and miserably, with no object but somehow to make what was already at hand suffice for him. Against this insidious ill chance there exists no defense, since so often what today is detested will appear to-morrow—though surely still detestable—good and wise.

When he had finally, torch in hand, made his way down into the basement, this last sloth of weariness and impairment of too difficult desire was already infecting Mr. Lecky. Walking morosely, brooding in the bad light, he felt no animation in his wish to get silverware or even cooking pots. His dejection might have sent him up empty-handed, had not his indecisive torch beam, sweeping through the thicket of frames—folding wood, strung line, metal rod—on which clothes could be dried after washing, showed him suddenly a pile of oblong packages.

These were lengths of light rope drawn in neat, narrow loops, tightly coiled around, to be used for the same purpose as the frames where space was less constricted. Concerned, discouraged, as Mr. Lecky had been by the thought of endless burdens on his back, he was now refreshed. All was changed by the unexpected, opportune idea. With the aid of a line he could do his climbing unimpeded and at the top draw after him fairly heavy loads.

The packages, he learned from the paper encircling them, contained each twenty yards. With no exact idea, nor means of forming one, Mr. Lecky guessed that three, or, to be safe, four lengths would be enough. Joined together they ought certainly to extend from the ninth floor to the bottom of the stair shaft. He dropped them over his shoulder into the pack basket.

For his kitchen utensils it was necessary to go to those counters toward the front. Among them, he selected and added to the rope several saucepans. A frying pan and a small kettle he might find occasion to use. Thus laden, he turned back, went down in the dark and up the stairs by which he had entered.

Of the things Mr. Lecky had come down to get, only the silverware for him to eat with remained. Yet, back here, close to the department in which he had found drugs and toilet goods, he thought of something else. With the apparent irrelevance of desires not consciously countenanced making themselves conscious, he recalled his experiment with the witch-hazel extract.

Still sure that it was not wholesome, feeling, too, a conviction hard for him to explain, of the enormity of attempting to hearten or warm himself with a preparation not intended for that purpose, Mr. Lecky presently found the shelf and took down a second bottle for his pack. Whether he would or would not drink it, he did not have to settle now. He left the settlement for a time when he might much more greatly desire to drink it.

Mr. Lecky turned toward the silverware department, and so toward the stairs in front. This he had planned to do, and this he was doing; but as he walked, his mind stiff and discordant in the minor struggle between defiance and guilt about the bottle, he thought how strangely and frequently he came back to this spot. It was no more than chance, but Mr. Lecky, though he thought nothing of one chance event, could find cause for a grievous and disturbing doubt in chance operating the same way too often.

Able to see the sinister, never-explained bell which must have been the one ringing yesterday, Mr. Lecky began, though vaguely and without concentrated attention, to feel in his mind for a relation of circumstances; and one at least he very soon saw, or thought he did. Nothing would have been more natural than, when the bell rang, for him to go and see what was desired. If he had done that, he would have returned here more times still. Certainly it might be supposed—since now he remembered well having felt it before—that a reason existed for him to come, and some grave instinct, unable to communicate with him logically, worked in this way to overcome his stupidity and blindness, to call his attention to what he must by no means fail to see.

Distressed by his ingenious, uncomfortable idea of something very urgent, momentous, vital, which perhaps he was steadily not seeing, Mr. Lecky stared about him. He even considered inspecting his idiot. So horrid and senseless an impulse he resisted; and, feeling the irrational tug strongly inherent always in gruesome things, he was annoyed. Once annoyed, he saw that the whole matter could be solved by giving himself no more opportunities for fancy. He ought to take care to have no occasion for coming downstairs again for a long time.

Stepping behind a show case and opening it, Mr. Lecky picked up forks, spoons, a knife less dangerous than the one he had been using upstairs; but his resolve to be long coming back suggested a larger supply. Like china, silverware must either be cleaned or discarded. By taking one of the weighty oblong chests, ostentatiously open inside the case to show its trays of nested silver pieces, he would supply himself for weeks. It might be difficult to carry so heavy a load up step by step, but here he could usefully employ his rope.

Choosing a chest and lugging it to the stair shaft, Mr. Lecky turned the key in its small lock. Setting down his basket, he took out a package of rope and fastened one end to the bar handle set in a plate with sockets on the lid. For his purpose Mr. Lecky would have found two half hitches simple and serviceable, but how greatly could trifling matters plague him, for he had never learned to tie knots properly. What he improvised was a distorted tangle, an impromptu invention of his own. Tugging it, he considered it satisfactory. Presented next with the need to join ends, he was inevitably incapable of making a true square knot, but what he did make again seemed to him all right. Soon he had four lengths united.

He was, as always, some time in gaining the ninth floor. Winded, he rested a few minutes, taking the precaution of fastening the rope end to the rail. Peering over, he could see the length of it swaying far down to the small chest on the paving at the bottom. When his breath was recovered, he began to haul up, hand over hand.

The chest was, to be sure, heavy. The oscillating circle which it started to describe strained his arms. The moving rope frayed the skin of his palms. Yet he had lifted it more than halfway, the coils of line accumulating on the floor beside him, and, encouraged, he pulled faster. A few additional moments, and he might have succeeded; but already the rope's unlimber newness was stealthily facilitating the slipping of the second bad knot. Suddenly it ran faster. For one helpless instant Mr. Lecky could feel the accident impending. The line eased, sprang slightly, swung free. Falling five stories, the chest landed in an appalling crash of broken wood and scattered silver on stone pavement.

In his indignation, Mr. Lecky stood breathing heavily, more inclined to blame the perversity of the rope than his own now proved ineptitude. Indeed, the failure of his plan seemed to him, as he stood there, to have a possible significance which angered him as much as the accident. He had attempted to get up a chest only because of his determination to insure himself against another descent. Even the fact that he had in his pockets pieces enough for his use, and so needed to go down no more than he intended to, did not wholly reassure him. He lifted up his pack basket mournfully and went into the dining-room. Here he did what he could to forget the matter.

EIGHT

The Evening at Home

MR. LECKY WASTED time preparing his dinner, and was in no hurry while he ate it, but he wanted less of it than he had prepared. Attempting to heat a whole tinned chicken, he removed it from its container and put it in a saucepan, but he was successful in really warming only one side of it. Water had to be fetched from the lavatory and he had filled his kettle full. Over so small and unsteady a flame this was too great a quantity to boil soon. Impatient, he found the powder which boiling water was said to change to coffee unpalatable. These annoyances delayed and interrupted him; but even so, Mr. Lecky had started his meal too early. When he was done, instead of being night, it was still late afternoon.

The sunlight, sadly descending, had first to pass the outer windows. Diluted, it came then through the false casements of the dining-room. With it were traces of the original warmth and incomparable glow, but they were windless, enclosed—heat and light without any life left. This melancholy illumination reflected up from the table contributed pallor only to Mr. Lecky's unshaven face. The slanting shafts, the last sunbeams, barely brought out the dust motes in the air. Universal silence, not right for daytime, was impregnate with the inactivity of disuse, vacancy, human desertion.

To replace the stimulation of crowds and to dispense with the comforts of human companionship a well-stocked mind is said to serve. A disordered one probably serves much better, for few sane men are hermits and few hermits are very long sane. In any event, Mr. Lecky was without a well-stocked mind, as he was without further incentive to action. To clear up the small dreary litter, dispose of the torn-open cans and the soiled utensils left from the miserable preparation of his dinner would only take a moment. Having so little to do, Mr. Lecky could see no reason to start doing it. Instead, he got up, leaving everything. Coming out into the aisle which communicated with his various rooms, he went down to the bedroom. In the extremities of boredom he often tried reading, had once or twice found real solace that way.

In the bedroom the more extensive curtains and perhaps the relative placing of the hidden outside windows made it almost dark. To read at all, Mr. Lecky would need a light. Drawing the most comfortable of the chairs close to the dressing table, he lit two large tapers, placed them erect and close together by his device of the spilled wax. When their flames had grown full and steadied, he took his book and opened it.

Mr. Lecky read with the careful slowness of a person little given to reading. He read slower even than usual, for the text was difficult and wordy; but on the other hand, he could soon conclude that, even as he had hoped when he saw the indecent jacket, he was sure to find material of some interest. Afraid that he might miss it in this maze of words if he skipped any, Mr. Lecky read doggedly, paragraph by paragraph, page by page.

Perhaps now it was night.

Wondering, Mr. Lecky showed how little this hopeful reading held him. Outside it was as good as dark, and having got up and seen it, he came back; but he did not sit down or take his book again. He stood bemused, rubbing his chin. Finally he looked at the two bottles on the bureau.

When he reached the dining-room, Mr. Lecky set up and lit another candle. He cleared the remains of his meal away, at least as far as the chest top. Now he had a glass available, but he poured only a little of the liquid from the bottle into it. So little might be supposed to be less harmful, if harm resulted from the drinking. Since none at all would in obvious fact be least harmful, Mr. Lecky was not easy. He smelled it. He tasted it. At last, irresolute, he drank it. This was no sooner done than he regretted the impulse. He stood tense, waiting for it to cause him great pain.

It caused him nothing but a feeling of warmth in his stomach, so after a while, he would seem justified in drinking more, if he wished to, hoping to enjoy greater warmth. Mr. Lecky was not so easily persuaded. That would perhaps be enough for tonight. If no ill came of it, he might, tomorrow night, try more. He would go back and read a little longer.

Bending forward, Mr. Lecky had been about to blow out his candle, but it occurred to him that he did not need to. Light from this source could be squandered; on the seventh floor he had seen candles in immense quantities. He might even, if he chose, illuminate several rooms; and such a plan seemed to him cheerful. He would put candles in the rooms separating his bedroom from the dining-room. Thus he had presently an agreeable glow in the too feminine, orchid, green and yellow bedroom, and in a living-room of some formal elaborateness. The lighting of the living-room showed him a chair more comfortable than the one he had been sitting in. If he read again, he would do it here.

Seated soon in this better chair with his book and the candlelight arranged to fall on it, Mr. Lecky discovered one thing not to his liking. If he lifted his eyes they inevitably met a mirror centered over a stiff, slight sofa. At this angle the glass did not show him himself. Instead, he saw one lighted edge of the wide-open fourth side of the room. Dimmer light reached the crowded furniture across the aisle. More and more indistinct, the angles and edges of rows behind the first disappeared gradually into a darkness of great depth or extent. Without moving or meaning to look, Mr. Lecky found himself keeping in this way an unwanted watch on the night-filled floor. The frame of the mirror held this view like an important picture; perhaps an unfinished one whose insignificant and subordinated background was first filled in. It lacked only the thing or person of which it was intended to be a portrait.

By degrees the vacancy of the mirror took more of Mr. Lecky's attention than he gave the printed page. He got up, walked a few steps until he stood opposite the glass. Now the background became the softly lighted wall, and against it he saw himself standing incredulous, for he looked worse than he would have thought, more sinister and unkempt. The mirror, too, attacked his reality, reduced him to a thin image, living, but somehow hardly human, dangerously gross and big in his ill-fitting new suit. This perfect representation would prove to be glass if you advanced and felt it with your fingers. It would prove to be nothing if you stepped a yard aside. The candlelight, up from the table behind, seemed white in reflection, or gray white. Shadows falling forward on Mr. Lecky's face made his eyes look empty and senseless; his face, already soiled with the beard he had begun, was etiolated, exhausted of blood.

No picture was better than one so ugly and disturbing. Restless, Mr. Lecky turned away. He had nowhere to go but to the dining-room, and there he had nothing to do.

This time, Mr. Lecky thought, he must feel better. The dose had been heroic. In his stomach the reddened membranes heated him vitally; his heart drew longer on the beat, squeezed the blood of his life out harder, and so he did feel better. He need not drink any more.

He continued to sit still at the table, for his distracting restlessness was, little by little, becoming dissipated. The longer he sat, the less there remained of it. In its place grew a content, founded not ignobly on mere ease and security, but on slowly and newly felt great reserves of courage and carelessness, reminding him of how relatively well off he was, how much he owned. It made him lordly, positive in his attention, capable of sound quick decisions. After a while he arose, thinking of his book with more relish.

Glancing, as he passed it, at the draped silk and soft colors of the smaller, rejected bedroom, he could notice details not before, nor now, important, but now interesting. His observation was incisive; he saw and liked everything. This bed was made up as though to sleep in. The cover was turned back to show the fine lavender tone of the blankets. They were in turn folded over to show the sheets tinted pale green. An elongated seat or couch, having a support for the back at one end only, was set across the room's far corner. It contained, he saw now, several round satin cushions. Against them lay an ornamental doll with painted face and spineless body, legs angled out under a rich little dress of silk and lace.

The doll pleased Mr. Lecky. Stepping in, he rearranged it to correct its boneless attitude of soft exhaustion. Seeing it set up, he liked it better immodestly prostrated, as it had first been, and touched it back. Now he examined the walls and was taken at once by an unnoticed trio of oval, terra-cotta masks affixed as decorations. Light from the big candle he had placed on the dressing table shone on their glazed surfaces; but under that their broad blunt features were warm-colored. They looked out narrow-eyed, drowsy, as though hung up still in a languor from some sustained obscenities.

But, alas, the fronts of faces only, as the beautiful debauched doll was only stuffed cloth.

Mr. Lecky sat on the edge of the bed a moment, staring back at them. Fancy, considering them, was freer here. The complicated art of reading did not interrupt. Mr. Lecky thought with clarity of women, whole and actual.

More real in this use than any exactly named or definitely remembered face was the immense store of impressions, the glimpses, the aggregation of numberless forgotten or unnoticed turns of desire when unchastened fancy wasted its minute on a wish too sudden and untimely for possible fulfillment.

Mr. Lecky sat there on the ornate, to him, beautiful,

bed, a hand resting on the turned-back sheets, relishing the suggestion that some woman would presently retire to this expensive room and go to bed. Imagining what she might look like, he suffered from the surfeit of faces he would like her to have—none could be too high or too low, none too beautiful or too scornful.

Once fitted to this intimacy, the color of eyes, the tones of hair, individual details of expression, of speech or gesture, he could make free with all women, find in them all a charm not airy like the word and trifling, but rank and vital, sinking through his warm breast, rooted in the quick, fed on the sap of his bowels where the alcohol inflamed them. In this happy stupor he brooded over his imaginary guests, undressing. Their individual deft ways of slipping off a stocking, or stepping out of a dress, absorbed him. He saw the candle-light and the shadows on their serene bare flesh before they re-clothed themselves to sleep. One followed another; they arrived with grace and he observed them. They took down their hair, if they had hair possible to take down, did whatever they considered necessary with the toilet articles spread out on the bright dressing table, slipped into bed; slept, he could presume.

> *. . . we easily know*
> *By this these angels from an evil sprite*
> *Those set our hairs, but these our flesh upright.*

Time was passing over him, and with its passing Mr. Lecky felt a faraway numbness. Slowly, do what he would, he was forgetting these women, he was disinclined to concentrate. Arising, he went back to the table in the dining-room and filled his glass.

Movement, or more drink, seemed to restore, though

in a mood altogether passive, the earlier acuteness of thought and feeling. Creeping up on Mr. Lecky, seeping up from his stomach, came the fine awareness of a horizon enlarged. Less graphic, this mood took away his need to stir himself or find anything to do. He was happy merely to sit there in the dining-room with his glass. He was calmed by the freedom and meditative scope of tranquil distances. At peace in his seat, at peace he could be, too, in a whole imaginary realm where he had access, effortless and unlimited. What this kingdom contained that was so valuable he did not have to know. Indeed, it contained nothing which could be known; it was formed entirely of undefined possibilities. Named, or in any way pushed toward fact, they would cease to exist. To Mr. Lecky, drinking, it seemed very likely that henceforth, from this time on, he would have the intelligence to live here. He would not allow himself to return to the disappointing past, nor submit to any detestable present.

This was such a good thing, coming indubitably out of his glass, that more drink ought to bring him things even better. Anxious to enjoy them, Mr. Lecky reached for the bottle. Pouring, he spilled a little, for he was very drunk.

NINE

The Familiar Face

SOMETIME MR. LECKY had left the dining-room. The candles had burned themselves to flat pools in which the last fragments of the wicks fell over and drowned. Starting to remove his clothes to go to bed, Mr. Lecky had never finished, and though he slept profoundly, he did not sleep at ease.

Coming to consciousness he was afflicted by an immense misery of pain and sickness. Though he had not slept long, he had drunk late, so there was a gloom of day, sullen, without sun. His distress hardly let him think, but such dreariness might mean rain outdoors.

Mr. Lecky lay motionless; the misery of his body absorbed him. He might, he supposed, feel better soon. He could lie quiet, probably sleep.

Now that he thought of seeking it again, he did not like sleep. Relinquishing himself to that nothingness, though safely done ten thousand times, had never convinced him. It was always too much like death, and more like it than ever now. The laboring ill-ease that woke him up remained. A subconsciousness, a kind of fibered awareness, let him feel his physical being, travailing and heavy laden, doing all it could.

Feeling this, it was possible to feel deeply if not clearly how little more might be too much. All the amazing resources, the infinite, sensitive and skillful compensations, the incredible faculties for repair, would prove too slow or too minute. There would be a last frantic effort, an embargo on the wasted energy of consciousness. In this coma, matters would go, however, from bad to worse. Even indispensable processes must slow and stop. Perhaps there would be a moment's complete halt, an utter end to activity; but most cells would be for a long while still living, ignorant of the disaster until the hectic microscopic carnival of decay burst in on them. Only bones would be left when this concluding liveliness was ended.

Mr. Lecky, well enough, if unwillingly, aware of the rot sometime awaiting him, was disgusted to think of his good flesh so reduced. The certainty of its end made it prematurely loathsome. It was foul stuff—wretched man, to be so amply provided with it! It was the means of his horrid predestination. It consigned Mr. Lecky to the extinction he abhorred; it marked him, still living, for putrefaction. Who should deliver him from the body of this death?

Mr. Lecky suffered, with the thought of his end, the stripping of himself to solitude. Here he developed nothing; he only saw what he had. His isolation in skull and breast had advanced with his unfolding in the womb. Before there was a consciousness to be incarcerated, its prison was built. There separate and single-handed consciousness grew up. For cold comfort Mr. Lecky could have the assurance that no man was lonelier or less lonely than any other, than himself. From his terrible fastness, Mr. Lecky signaled, a doubtful solace, with his voice. Back over a void more absolute than the width of the world came to his ears the faint halloos in kind. Locked up for life, he had no life, no friends, no servant but his slovenly body. Humbled by thought, Mr. Lecky might see himself as only the whole shadow, sum of those part shadows, his past years; but seen by others, the whole of him came to less. All of him there was could be found in the industrious fomenting cesspool of his guts, the oxidation sack of lungs and appended heart, the cavity packed with a few pounds of the soft moist protoplasmic mass of his brain. Whatever their lonely efforts, like children making playmates of trees and rocks, his fellow-men at most imagined themselves in him, did to him as they would be done by. In ultimate fact, they were completely and helplessly indifferent. They passed by on the other side. Looking over, if they did, they saw Mr. Lecky, too, passing; him, too, remote, deep in himself, indifferent.

On the wide bed, Mr. Lecky, gross and disheveled, stirred moaning, put his hands on the mattress, half pushing himself up. He thought of going to his lavatory; but even as he moved, shaky with pain and illness, he heard an intolerable well-known sound far away in the store.

> *Deliver me from mine enemies, O God:*
> *defend me from them that rise up against me.*
> *Deliver me from the workers of iniquity,*
> *and save me from the bloody men.*

Desiring to keep him in where he could rest and at leisure realize his misery, his hopelessness, the great terror of being where he was, Mr. Lecky's mind resisted somewhat.

Yet, staggering to his feet, he passed groaning down the line of his rooms. Out he went by the stair door. His perfidious body conveyed him; it was, as he had always known, his enemy. This personal Judas, gone to the adversary, took everything. Mr. Lecky was left with no means to quit himself like a man. He had no feet to plant, no muscles to tug back, no hands to catch at passing holds.

He had no body to sweat and quake, no superfluous saliva to swallow. He held the rail of the stairs, fearing that terrible fall; and quickly, step by step, he reduced it.

Now he put behind him, toys, games, sporting goods, musical instruments, cameras. This was the eighth floor.

Rugs and carpets, upholstery fabrics, pillows, curtains, lamps, pictures, pottery, clocks. This was the seventh floor.

Groceries, glassware, china, table furnishings.

Men's wear, men's shoes, luggage, smoking supplies.

Boys', girls', and infants' apparel, baby carriages, nursery furniture. (He left no heirs of his body.)

Lingerie, negligees, corsets, cotton frocks, house dresses, women's and misses' outer apparel, furs. (His bed was empty, his house untended.)

Thrusting his face over the rail, Mr. Lecky saw that he would not fall far, if he fell, but he hastened. He did not wish to fall at all; and so he came out while the bell still rang. In the gloom of the dark day he could see the pale illuminated spark of its breaking circuit high on the pillar.

Now, under the bell, Mr. Lecky stopped, for the great gloom was deeper, and how could it be evening yet? From his pocket, thoughtless, he took his watch, looking at it lying in his hand. Still it said quarter past five; but as he would have put it back, remembering, he saw that it was going. The second hand progressed, marching its round, numbering the moments. In the dusk fallen at what he thought was noon, Mr. Lecky began to shake, while the bell sounded stridently on, peal after peal.

Who could be deaf to such ringing?

Mr. Lecky waited, and while his eyes ached in the gloom, he knew that no one could be; he heard that no one was.

Heavy the labor of climbing, awful the need to learn who went there, who rang, who must be met halfway! When you are dead it is hard to stand on your feet, to climb stairs, to keep your slit throat together; yet how that last was done Mr. Lecky now found out. You hold a hand upon your face to steady your head, and one upon your throat to close it, and step by step, you crawl until the top is reached and you can lie forward there.

Clutching the watch tight, Mr. Lecky, creeping, too, drew near. He stooped. Unwillingly, he took the idiot by the shoulder. Crouching as he turned up the fearful face, he bent his own face toward it, saw it again. His hand on the head, studying the uninjured side, Mr. Lecky beheld its familiar strangeness—not like a stranger's face, and yet it was no friend's face, nor the face of anyone he had ever met.

What this could mean held him, bent closer, questioning in the gloom; and suddenly his hand let go the watch, for Mr. Lecky knew why he had never seen a man with this face. He knew who had been pursued and cruelly killed, who was now dead and would never climb more stairs. He knew why Mr. Lecky could never have for his own the stock of this great store.